Seconds tic... ...countdown to nightmare

"I should have killed you before," Sakata Fuja sneered.

"You have the opportunity to try," Keio Ohara suggested to the karate-trained ninja death merchant.

Fuja attacked.

A vicious punch to the gut stole Keio's breath. But he countered, using his arm to stop his assailant's smooth stroke of death.

Keio, battling both enemy and time, moved quickly.

He delivered a high side kick to Fuja's face, then slashed with an arm in a cross-body stroke. That blow slammed the terrorist squarely in the throat.

His windpipe burst. He gargled his own blood.

Phoenix Force lives on!

PHOENIX FORCE

AN EXECUTIONER SERIES

Tigers of Justice

Gar Wilson

A GOLD EAGLE BOOK FROM

W⦵RLDWIDE

TORONTO · NEW YORK · LONDON

First edition April 1983

ISBN 0-373-61304-0

Special thanks and acknowledgment to William Fieldhouse
for his contributions to this work.

Printed in Canada

Yakov Katzenelenbogen—a French-Israeli intelligence veteran with one arm. Unbeatable in combat.

Gary Manning—a Canadian explosives engineer. Incredibly strong, he thrives on trouble.

Keio Ohara—a Japanese master of martial arts. Unusually tall. Unusually deadly.

David McCarter—a British brawler, famous for his SAS activities. Rude. Rugged. Ruthless.

Rafael Encizo—a Cuban survivor of Castro's prisons, expert in underwater warfare. Altogether fearless.

Phoenix Force is Mack Bolan's five-man army that fights the dirtiest of wars. They trust, respect and care deeply for each other, bonded by the extremes of their combat experiences. They are all-action.

Dedicated to James Brady, former press secretary
to President Ronald Reagan, who was seriously wounded
when caught in the wrong place at the wrong time.
Victims of the barbarism of the unhinged are reminders
of the high cost of our naivety in the hellgrounds.

1

The Quinton Nuclear Plant was nicknamed the Taj Mahal by its employees. If one was terribly nearsighted, a resemblance to the famous Indian building could be seen in the huge white dome between two enormous gray silos. The Quinton plant housed the turbogenerators that produced electricity for the greater part of Quinton County, Indiana. Under the half sphere lurked one of the most awesome and controversial inventions in the technological history of mankind—a nuclear reactor.

Although Bob Driscoll was aware that the atomic furnace had more destructive potential than a thousand pounds of TNT, he seldom considered the hazards of an accident. Perched in his guard tower, a structural dwarf compared to the generator silos, the six-foot-three, 260-pound ex-policeman had little contact with the technicians and supervisors who filed in and out of the plant. Maybe the other security guards at the personnel gate and the office building fretted about such things, but not Big Bob.

The scientists who operated the plant seemed to

know what they were doing. Dr. Lambert, who had more fancy degrees than a five-dollar whore has johns, personally assured Driscoll the reactor couldn't blow up. It *could* have what they called a meltdown. Driscoll didn't really understand what that meant, but he knew a meltdown would cause radioactive fallout to leak all over Indiana. No sweat. Lambert told him they'd built about a hundred safety devices into the plant.

After Three Mile Island caused such a fuss, the Quinton installation had beefed up its emergency equipment to make the place accident proof. They had safety valves for the safety valves and backup generators for the backup generators, in case anything malfunctioned. Hell, the plant was as sound as a dollar *used* to be.

Big Bob didn't worry about being turned into a uniformed Pop Tart by an atomic accident; his job was security. A former Indianapolis cop, he saw enough sickies in his twenty years with the force to know there were crazies who'd like to blow up a nuclear plant just to get even with the world—a world they resented for one reason or another. Some weirdo terrorist groups might even want to break in and steal some uranium to build a homemade atom bomb. As if that wasn't bad enough, the workers had to be checked to make sure they weren't smuggling out radioactive material or classified files to sell to such nuts.

That's why the Quinton security officers were paid

almost ten times better than the average rent-a-cop. This was no doorknob-rattling job. Driscoll's station that night was in the tower on the north side of the installation. The guards alternated assignments to prevent boredom. Watching the area from the perch was a monotonous chore that did not seem necessary, since a steel fence surrounded the compound. If anybody touched or cut the barrier, they'd trigger an electrical alarm system that set off more bells than Notre Dame cathedral. As an additional precaution, there were sensors within the compound to warn if anything bigger than a rabbit got through the fence.

So why have a guy watching the place from the crow's nest? The security supervisor didn't believe in taking any chances, that's why. Some psycho with a homemade grenade launcher or a professional terrorist could still position himself outside the fence and lob some HE shells into the plant. A while ago a group of mercenaries on some sort of training mission wandered pretty damn close to a nuclear plant in Florida before the sheriff's department caught them. In this crazy world anything could happen. . . .

''What the hell?'' Driscoll muttered when he saw, out of the corner of his eye, something move.

Turning from the magazine centerfold on the desk in the guard shack, he rose from his swivel chair. Driscoll's hand dropped to the .357 Ruger on his hip as he stared out the screen window. Floodlights illuminated the compound, revealing nothing. The fence remained untouched by anything but blackness. A cloud must have passed over the moon and thrown a shadow on the area. Driscoll shrugged and returned to his seat. He opened his thermos and poured himself a cup of sugar-laced coffee. *Must be getting tired,* he thought. *I've got the willies for some dumb-ass reason.*

Driscoll sipped the hot black liquid as he glanced down at the beautiful naked female displayed on the pages before him. How does a guy get to make it with a woman like that, he wondered. Bob's wife had got fat and sloppy and indifferent about sex. He'd sure like to screw a woman who didn't feel like a rubber mannequin. . . .

Then he heard it. A harsh scratching sound. Metal on stone.

More puzzled than concerned, the rent-a-cop turned to look outside. His mouth fell open when he saw the dark outline of a man's head and shoulders at the window. Hard almond-shaped eyes stared back at him from a face otherwise concealed by black cloth.

Driscoll's hand flew to his revolver, his muscles and nerves responding to the threat while his mind wondered how the hell the man in black had got to the window. There was no fire escape, and the only stairs were built within the tower. He couldn't have put up a ladder that quickly, and a grappling hook would have sounded like a howitzer on the aluminum-plated roof. The walls were smooth concrete. No one could just climb up it with his bare hands, for chrissake!

The guard's gun never cleared leather. With a hiss the man at the window tore open the screen by a single slash of his gloved palm. He then leaped through the opening and attacked. Driscoll caught a glimpse of the dark curved blades in the black hand that swung toward him. Sharp metal struck the guard under the chin. Blood splashed across his pale blue shirt; Big Bob Driscoll staggered backward into his desk. He vaguely realized his throat had been ripped open before he slumped to the floor and died.

The night crew at the Quinton plant consisted of thirty-nine employees, including security personnel and a custodian. Most of the men and women on duty, however, were technicians trained to operate the monstrous nuclear reactor. The bulk of these individuals were located in the main control room. Four technicians and two guards were posted in the basement. Workers in white smocks wearily watched the air-pressure valves and radiation meters registering the intensity of the glowing uranium beast that raged inside the central core of the complex.

Wayne Kessler, a Quinton security patrolman stationed at the basement entrance, glanced up from his tuna-salad sandwich when the electrical door hummed open. The door was operated by a coded button system, like a push-button telephone. One had to press the correct sequence of numbers to open it. He almost choked on a mouthful of tuna and bread when he saw three figures, dressed entirely in black with hoods and scarves covering their faces, at the threshold.

Before Kessler could reach for his weapon or the alarm button under his desk, one of the intruders raised a pistol. The guard stared into the black hole at the end of a metal sausage attached to the gun barrel. A harsh cough accompanied a burst of flame from the muzzle of the silencer. Kessler's forehead split open when a .380-caliber projectile tunneled deeply into his brain.

The guard's lifeless body toppled from the chair. Technicians gasped in horror as the three armed shadows charged forward.

Barry Gibb, the surviving security officer, clawed at his holstered Magnum. A black-garbed assailant raised his arm high and snapped it down like the tail of a striking scorpion. A dark steel sliver whistled through the air and slammed point first into the guard's chest. Gibb cried out, stumbled and fell to one knee. The metal spike jutted from the center of his bloodied uniform shirt. He tried to pull the projectile from his flesh, but failed and collapsed limply on the floor.

Sandra Michaels, a technician, screamed as the silenced .380 whispered. Her open mouth caught a flat-nosed bullet that burned through a vertebra before it burst the base of her skull, severing her spinal column. Arthur Jennings reached for the wall alarm. Three slugs punched into his chest, pounding the technician's corpse the length of the control panel.

Mel Jackson, the senior operator, seized a curve-backed plastic chair for an improvised weapon. His valiant effort proved futile as one of the invaders swiftly moved in and launched a karate side kick to Jackson's chest. The blow sent the technician hurtling into the control panel. With a *kiai* shout the assailant chopped the hard edge of his hand into the operator's lower abdomen. Jackson's guts were ripped apart. He doubled over with a groan. His black-clad opponent quickly wrapped an arm around his neck and applied a headlock. He then slammed the heel of his palm into the side of Jackson's skull. Bone crunched. The killer released his victim, and Jackson crumpled to the floor, his neck broken.

Stu Smithers, the remaining technician, jerked his arms over his head in surrender. The sinister gunman stepped forward, elevated his pistol and plastered Smithers between the eyes.

As silent as the shadows they resembled, two of the invaders inspected the bodies while the third watched the entrance, his silenced Beretta held ready. Satisfied the victims were dead, the leader removed a black ditty bag from his shoulder and extracted a small RDX mine. Designed to disable ships and submarines, the gray disk contained a waterproof timer and detonator and four ounces of plastic explosives.

Placing the magnetized bomb to the panel, the demolitions man calmly turned the switches of the air-pressure valves. He then activated the mine. The trio exchanged nods and quickly left the basement control room. After the door hummed shut, another mine was attached to the button-operated lock. They hurried to the emergency stairwell. The first explosion would occur in ten minutes.

"Holy shit!" Leonard Barlow exclaimed when the red lights popped across the main control panel like a string of Christmas-tree ornaments. "The goddamn rods are rising!"

Baron control rods were used to start the atom-splitting process within the reactor core. After it began, the rods were lowered and held in place by an air-pressure system. Something serious had gone wrong, and the fission process was escalating at a faster rate.

"How many rods are up?" Thomas Herter, the head supervisor, demanded.

The technician's face paled as he turned to Herter and said, "*All* of them!"

"Christ!" The supervisor dashed to the interplant phone on the wall and punched the number to the basement. "Those stupid bastards must have left the valves open."

"How could they have left them all open?" Barlow wondered aloud. "Isn't anybody paying any attention to their panels? They must be having an orgy down there."

"Nobody's answering the phone," Herter stated. "I'm going to see what's wrong."

A loud bang joined the wail of alarm sirens. Although everyone in the control room realized it was physically impossible for the reactor to literally explode, the sound sent chills of terror up their backbones. Herter raced to the elevator, and the others stared at the galvanometer. The gauge registered the electrical current produced by the reactor turbogenerators and confirmed that the power level was soaring to an uncontrollable degree.

"That uranium is going to burn the reactor's guts out at this rate," Joe Lincoln, an engineer who had helped construct the reactor vessel, remarked. "If that son of a bitch melts down, we can all say, 'Hello, China!'"

When uranium or any nuclear fuel melts, it becomes highly unstable and dangerous. No substance can reliably stop it; thus the theory of the China Syndrome evolved. Molten radioactive fuel could conceivably burn through the bottom of the reactor and into the earth, all the way to China.

The deadly substances would also seep into the atmosphere. Radiation poisons vary in nature from devastating alpha, beta and gamma rays to the insidious strontium 90, which destroys human bone cells. No one can predict how many lives would be lost if such elements broke free of the confines of the reactor.

"Hell," Barlow muttered. "None of us will be alive to see China!"

Supervisor Herter returned, his expression grim. "The controls to the basement door have been blasted apart. We'll have to burn our way in with a torch."

"For God's sake, Tom!" Lincoln exclaimed. "There isn't time for that! The reactor's going to melt down like a goddamn ice-cream cone in a microwave oven!"

"Isn't there an emergency air-pressure system for the control rods?" asked Janet Tolo, another technician, desperation in her voice.

"Yeah," Lincoln snorted. "In the basement control center."

"I'm calling Paxon," Herter announced, referring to the general manager of the Quinton plant.

"Screw Paxon!" the engineer snapped. "We've got to shut that reactor down. Paxon thinks in dollars and cents. He'll expect us to hold back a nuclear meltdown with chewing gum and chicken wire. We need Lambert."

The galvanometer continued to record their approaching doom, the needle swinging faster and faster as the uranium furnace reached a critical level. Herter found Dr. Daniel Lambert's home phone number.

"Hello?" the physicist said.

Herter explained what had happened, fighting to keep panic from his words. "We're sitting on an atomic powder keg, doctor. . . ."

"Is the coolant system intact?" Lambert asked calmly.

Sure, Herter thought. *Your ass is in bed fifty miles away!* but said, "The primary one is, but the emergency system is buried in the basement."

"You couldn't cool that uranium at this stage with a thousand coolant systems," Barlow commented, hearing Herter's reply.

"Fine," Lambert said. "Dump the water out of the reactor immediately."

"Dump the water!" Herter nearly dropped the telephone receiver. "The core is about to melt down and you want us to *dump* the water coolant?"

"What the hell's the matter with you, Herter?" Lincoln snapped. "This is a heavy-water reactor. The water itself is radioactive. Sure, it cools the reactor. But it also produces the fission within the core. Drain that sucker and you kill the fission and stop the chain reaction."

"But that's dangerous. . . ." Herter began.

"Sure it is," the engineer agreed. "I helped put that reactor vessel together, remember? I know dumping the water can cause a vacuum, and the belly of the bastard might fall in. Then we'd have a China Syndrome. But what the hell do you think we'll have if we don't do it?"

"I heard Joe and he's right," Lambert said. "Dump the water and pray the vessel holds."

Joe Lincoln had already crossed the room to the coolant panel. He threw on the reactor's drain switch. Herter felt resentment mixed with relief that someone else had taken the responsibility from his shoulders. Barlow crossed his fingers. Janet crossed herself. All eyes turned to the reactor pressure gauge.

"If that vessel collapses, you're fired, Joe," Herter said with a weak smile.

Lincoln grinned stiffly in reply.

Tons of heavy water poured from the reactor into the containment area built into the main vessel. The pressure gauges rose alarmingly, causing fears that the gasholder, the lid of the reactor, might burst, spilling radioactive death. Then the pressure declined.

"Galvanometer dropping," Barlow announced. "The fission is dying down."

"So are the turbogenerators," Herter noticed. "Quinton County will be without electricity the rest of the night."

"At least there'll still be a Quinton County," Lincoln said.

The pair looked at each other and solemnly nodded.

2

The men sitting at the rectangular table in a conference room in the Justice Department headquarters in Washington, D.C. had read the report concerning the incident at the Quinton Nuclear Power Plant. No one spoke, however, as Dr. Lambert concluded his statement.

"Of course, the plant has shut down until all damage is repaired," the weary physicist told the meeting. "When we burned through the door of the basement control center, we found everyone inside was murdered. The air-pressure valves were deliberately left open, and the controls were destroyed by some sort of explosive."

"Thank you, doctor," said Wade Sommer, the lantern-jawed special investigator for the Justice Department.

Lambert sat between Sommer and two representatives from the Nuclear Regulatory Commission—NRC—and the Nuclear Research and Development Administration—NRDA. At the opposite side of the table were five strikingly different individuals. Sommer had quickly introduced him to them, but Lambert suspected the names they used were false. He had no idea he was in the same room with the most unique and highly trained "foreign legion" of antiterrorist mercenaries in the world: Phoenix Force.

"The lab report said the explosives were Composition-4," commented Gary Manning, the demolitions expert, folding his arms across his barrel chest. "That's not your run-of-the-mill pipe bomb."

"Well," said David McCarter, the tall Englishman seated next to Gary, "ordinary terrorists—whatever they are—don't break into atomic installations." He smiled thinly, enhancing the foxlike appearance of his lean handsome face with its long brown sideburns and trimmed mustache.

"That's what worries us, gentlemen," Harrison Reed, the representative from the NRC declared, jerking his steel-rimmed glasses from the bridge of his long nose. "How did they break in?"

"We were called in to answer that question," Yakov Katzenelenbogen replied. A heavyset man in middle age, the Israeli didn't appear to be one of the most efficient and highly trained antiterrorists in the world. His short-cropped gray hair, friendly blue eyes and his right arm—amputated at the elbow— presented a harmless image. Nothing was further from the truth.

"We need to know why they did it, as well," Wade Sommer added.

"I believe we have that answer, Inspector," Professor Milton Cohen of the NRDA stated in a soft cultured voice. The short bald scientist continued. "The terrorists tried to cause a nuclear-reactor meltdown—and very nearly succeeded. If the Quinton installation didn't operate one of this country's few heavy-water reactors, dumping the water would not have stopped the fission or prevented the 'accident' the saboteurs wished to create."

"You're saying they wanted it to look like an accident?" Sommer asked. "But they left bullet-riddled bodies all over the place. How did they expect anyone to believe it wasn't deliberate?"

"They thought the meltdown would occur," said Keio Ohara, the tall, broad-shouldered Japanese member of the Phoenix team. Keio had recovered magnificently from his grievous chest wound in Phoenix Force's Atlantic encounter. He was in fine shape, and it showed. But his voice was hesitant, emphasizing his unfamiliarity with fluent English. "In which case there would have been nothing left to discover," he concluded.

"That is correct," Cohen said. "Concrete, steel, glass, human tissues would have been fused together by the 2000-degree temperatures of a runaway meltdown. The entire site would have been reduced to a pile of radioactive slush."

"And the level would have been far more than the four hundred and fifty rads that are fatal to humans, yes?'' Keio added, using the nomenclature for radiation-absorption dose. ''This would make the area unsafe for any investigation for weeks.''

''Indeed,'' the NRDA man said. ''I see you know something about nuclear energy, young man.''

''I have some interest in the subject,'' Keio said, shrugging. ''My father was born in Hiroshima. He lost his family when they dropped the bomb.''

''How are they handling the situation at the Quinton plant, Dr. Lambert?'' Reed asked, shifting uncomfortably in his chair. The NRC concentrated on promoting peaceful uses for atomic power, and he didn't like anyone mentioning Hiroshima.

The physicist sighed. ''The blackout of Quinton County and the plant shutdown made it impossible to keep the incident from the public. General Manager Paxon told the press a malfunction occurred. He didn't mention several people were killed. But this can't be kept secret for long. The public is already upset about the accident, and they will certainly blame the deaths on a malfunction if they aren't told the truth.''

''Paxon was acting on the request of the Nuclear Regulatory Commission, doctor,'' Reed explained, adjusting his glasses. ''It's better if the general public believes this is an accident rather than terrorism. God, the panic we'd have....''

''A cover-up,'' Lambert said with disgust. ''The very thing we've always been accused of. It's also an insult to the men and women who have operated the Quinton plant safely for years.''

"I can understand your feelings, doctor," Cohen stated. "But in this case I'm inclined to agree with the NRC—and believe me, I seldom do."

"Believe him," Reed muttered sourly.

"I'm afraid a cover-up is necessary," Sommer added. "For now."

"That is, until we can make certain it won't happen again," Rafael Encizo, the fifth member of Phoenix Force said. The muscular, ruggedly handsome Cuban had been leafing through a copy of the incident report, content to listen to the others.

"Which brings us to the sixty-five-thousand-dollar question," McCarter declared, his London accent dissolving as he mimicked an American quiz-show host. "Whodunit?"

"There's another question that shouldn't be ignored," Rafael remarked, a long wrinkle creasing his forehead. "Will they try again—either at the Quinton plant or elsewhere?"

"I'd say there's a high probability they will," Yak said. "Everything suggests these terrorists are professionals—well organized, well armed and equipped and highly trained. That kind doesn't generally aim at a single target, and they're certainly not apt to give up because the first attempt failed."

"The first place to begin any investigation is at the scene of the crime," Gary said, leaning back in his chair. The Canadian was slow with gestures and words, but was quick with his mind and had lightning reflexes. In many ways Gary was a paradox. Although he loved the serenity of a forest, his workaholic nature cost him numerous friendships and one marriage. Physically and mentally he possessed enough endurance for six men.

Sommer nodded, agreeing to start the investigation at Quinton. "That's why we asked Dr. Lambert to join us. He'll be able to assist you at the Quinton plant."

"No sense in all five of us running to Indiana for that." Rafael shrugged. Attired in Levi's slacks and jacket, he toyed with a silver Pisces medallion that hung from his neck. Rafael wasn't born under that zodiac sign, and he personally regarded astrology as nonsense, but his current lady friend had given him the medallion, and it suited his nickname, *Pescado* or "fish." Rafael, an expert frogman, was as deadly as a killer whale. "I think we should split up and check out other likely targets for terrorists."

"Before you go poking about in nuclear power plants, I'd like to know what department of the government you five work for," Reed stated, irritation gripping his voice. "I assume you aren't with Mr. Sommer?"

"The Justice Department will be working with these gentlemen," Sommer explained. "I've been told to assist them with anything they may need. For example, I'll supply them with valid driver's licenses

and permits for weapons and special equipment anywhere in the United States.''

*And I hope the Bureau of Alcohol, Tobacco and
Firearms doesn't find out,* the Justice man thought.
*Christ, the Latino is the only naturalized U.S. citizen
of the group. These guys will be able to run all over
the country with machine guns, and they aren't even
Americans!*

"I was told to cooperate with them, too," Reed said.
"But before I start giving these men the necessary
paperwork to shuffle in and out of nuclear installations
as though they were supermarkets, I want to know what
authority they have. Don't you, Professor Cohen?''

The NRDA man calmly lit a curve-stemmed briar
pipe and replied, "I'm a scientist, not a bureaucrat.
These gentlemen are here to help us with a critical
problem. That's all I'm concerned about.''

Reed glared at Cohen.

"Mr. Reed," David McCarter began. A man
charged with nervous energy that bordered on hyper-
activity, McCarter methodically paced the floor.
"The United States has no official organization to
deal with terrorism on a national level. There are
SWAT teams trained to handle such things on local
and county levels—these chaps are quite good. But
this is too big for any police department to handle.
That's why we're here.''

"And," Yak added with a thin smile, "our authority comes from the Oval Office. Does *that* satisfy
you, Mr. Reed?''

The NRC representative woodenly nodded and busily examined the report forms as if he'd never seen them before. Actually, Phoenix Force had told him only part of the story. The president had been alerted about the Quinton Nuclear Power Plant incident. He, in turn, contacted the most incredible crime fighter in the history of the world—Mack Bolan, the Executioner. Now known as Colonel John Phoenix, the Executioner had not only survived his one-man war against the Mafia—he'd won. The man who had conquered impossible odds now took on an even greater challenge, pitting himself against international terrorism.

Even the Executioner, however, couldn't deal with all the fanatical groups that threatened America and the civilized world. But "Colonel Phoenix" was no longer alone in his new battle against the super barbarians. He'd picked five men, the best professional antiterrorists in the world, to serve as his strike team. The Executioner called on Phoenix Force to stop the world's terrorist animals.

"This is interesting," Gary Manning commented, glancing over the Quinton report. "Ballistics on the bullets removed from the victims state the projectiles were .380-caliber, flat-nosed, lead, wad cutters. No metal jackets. They expanded enough to appear to be 9mm slugs at first glance." The Canadian whistled softly. "One-hundred-and-twenty-grain bullets? That's a helluva load for a .380 to handle."

"Sounds like whoever throated the barrel of that pistol knows his business," Rafael remarked.

"Another grimly fascinating feature can be found in the autopsy report," Yak said. "Three of the victims were shot, one was pistol-whipped to death, one man's neck was broken, another's throat was ripped open and the last died from a small dirk dipped in curare."

"Have you seen this weapon?" K.O. asked, a trace of urgency in his voice.

"Yes," Sommer answered. "So did Dr. Lambert."

"Would you say it resembled a spike, like a heavy-bladed ice pick with the handle removed?" Keio asked.

"That's exactly what it looks like," Sommer confirmed. "Do you know what it is?"

Keio Ohara nodded. "It is a *shuriken* dart," he said. "And it suggests something that seems too incredible to even consider as a theory."

David gazed out the window at the tip of the Washington Monument, which jutted above the early-morning mist. He wondered if he'd have time to visit the famous structure and the other great buildings in the nation's capital.

"I thought the incredible had become rather commonplace with us," the Englishman mused.

"If we are dealing with what I suspect," K.O. answered flatly, "it is quite unlike anything we have faced before."

3

The crowd at the front gate of the Quinton plant held signs protesting nuclear energy, supporting solar power and urging mankind to reject atomic insanity. The protestors included teenagers, senior citizens, housewives and businessmen from as far away as New York.

No entertainment personalities or political celebrities were present to attract media interest. No passionate cries of, "No more nukes!" filled the air. The demonstrators were silent as a small Oriental with dark sad eyes and a brooding expression stood at the podium. A large poster behind him had the legend *Anzen Sekai*, with its English translation, "Safe World." In the center a black circle contained a toadstool-shaped gray cloud with a red slash through it.

"We are told nuclear energy is safe, clean and effective," Osato Goro said in flawless English. His strong deep voice seemed out of place with his slight form. "This is the reality of atomic technology!" He held up his hands dramatically to display the abnormal stumps at the root of each little finger.

Osato lowered his arms and his voice. "My parents were in Hiroshima when your government dropped the bomb. My father was with a unit of soldiers stationed outside the city. His face was burned black by the heat. His eyeballs melted in their sockets when he looked into the blast. Then the great mushroom rose over Hiroshima like an enormous headstone to signal the beginning of the end of the human race."

Osato sighed wearily. "Father died. My mother, however, survived the day hell fell from the sky. Mother was exposed to the radiation. It made her sick for many weeks. Her gums bled and her teeth fell out. Her hair shed like the skin of a snake. But the horror of nuclear poison did not stop there. It penetrated her womb and her unborn child."

He raised a six-fingered hand. "You can see the results."

The crowd mumbled sounds of sympathy, but Osato Goro silenced them with a shake of his head.

"Do not pity me," he insisted. "Others were far less fortunate than I. Children were born blind or crippled. Some had no arms or legs or their limbs were withered and malformed. These terrible mutations continue to this very day! They shall continue for the next two hundred years. That is why I shall never marry. I shall never have children, never claim a family."

The demonstrators remained silent. Tears formed in the eyes of many.

"This is not a curse from God or whatever term you care to use," Osato declared in an emotional voice, his tone similar to a fire-and-brimstone preacher. "It is not the result of heritable diseases or a natural disaster. It is the plight of the nuclear age!"

"No more nukes! No more nukes!" a young woman with braided long hair, owlish sunglasses and a multicolored T-shirt shouted. She stopped and looked sheepishly at her sandaled feet when no one joined her chant.

Osato Goro continued. "Your scientists—and scientists all over the world—tell us that atomic energy can be harnessed for industrial use. They speak of burning uranium as if it is coal. Private corporations are permitted to build plants such as this," he said, thrusting a finger at the Quinton installation. "This has a nuclear reactor that produces enough radioactive poisons to make Hiroshima look like a brushfire. How can any man claim such deadly products can be handled safely?"

"They can't be!" a pimple-faced youth answered rashly. "Three Mile Island proved that!"

"Three Mile Island was a relatively mild incident compared to some," the Japanese said, taking advantage of the boy's outburst to feed more information to the crowd. "There have been dozens of nuclear excursions, as the physicists call them. In 1952, a Canadian heavy-water reactor like the one housed in this plant malfunctioned and spilled thousands of gallons of radioactive water. The installation was a death trap for weeks. In 1957, a radiation leak in England spread contamination along the entire Cumberland coast. In 1961, three men were killed by a minor accident involving a reactor with a core only 3.7 decimeters square! A breeder reactor in Michigan almost had a runaway meltdown in 1966. Since a breeder produces plutonium containing the most deadly radioactive poisons, it could have contaminated an area for almost *five hundred thousand years*. The guardians of technology built the plant less than *thirty miles* from Detroit. The city, if not the entire state, could have been the victim of the worst nuclear disaster in history.''

The crowd voiced sounds of alarm and astonishment.

''Indeed,'' Osato smiled bitterly. ''Most of you were probably unaware of these incidents. They received little press coverage, thanks to the power of big business and its hold on your government. Such matters can be suppressed. Of course,'' he said, ''these cover-ups no longer occur. The reactor leak at Three Mile Island is proof of that, isn't it?''

The demonstrators reacted, anger building in their eyes.

''Yet how many of you recall an accident in 1979 at a nuclear plant in Kansas, where two men lost their lives?'' Osato asked. ''How many recall the fact that the Nuclear Regulatory Commission approved the construction of *two* nuclear plants along a fault line in Southern California in 1981? It seems equipment malfunctions and human error are not enough risk for the greedy, power-mad schemers involved in atomic energy. Now they must gamble with nature and hope their installations of death can withstand earthquakes, too!''

He folded his arms and sadly shook his head. "I do not place the blame for this sword of Damocles on your country—although the United States was, and *still is*, the leader in the insane race to utilize a power that should never have been created. All nations involved in nuclear research, including my own, must share the burden of guilt. It is their responsibility to bring an end to the heartless science of the atom— and our responsibility to see they do their duty for mankind.

"*Anzen Sekai* was formed by my associates and me to serve as the town crier for the world," he said, gesturing to a group of Orientals seated behind the podium. They wore conservative suits and plain ties, matching the somber expressions on their youthful faces. Most were under thirty, and all appeared physically fit. "We have seen the suffering of atomic bombs and radiation. *Anzen Sekai* has vowed to do everything in its power to prevent the tragedy of Hiroshima and Nagasaki from ever occurring again.

"The United Nations struggles to keep World War III from erupting. Your government tries—or at least it did under past administrations—to reduce the arms race between itself and the Soviet Union. These things are good, but they are not good enough. Bombs are not necessary when places like this—'' he turned to the Quinton plant ''—are allowed to exist. A raging inferno of radioactivity is locked within that building. There are literally thousands of installations like it throughout the world—powder kegs of nuclear death.

"Scientists can only offer us theories about the awesome consequences of a complete reactor meltdown. Thousands, if not millions, would surely die. If the so-called China Syndrome proves accurate, molten uranium could literally burn through the bottom of a plant to the very core of the earth. Who can predict the result of such an incredible jolt to our planet? A single full-scale meltdown could cause global destruction.

"Such a disaster almost happened here two days ago," Osato continued. "Once again your media suppressed the facts about the incident. We know something malfunctioned, but we are not told what went wrong. At least four persons employed by the Quinton plant have not been seen or heard from since this most recent nuclear accident. How many have died? How many more must die before the people of the world unite in one great collective voice and demand an end to nuclear power once and for all?"

Osato Goro sighed heavily, his shoulders drooping. The man's entire body sagged, as if weary from his battle against the dragons of atomic energy. "The choice is simple. We must save ourselves and future generations from the horrors of the nuclear age by bringing it to a permanent halt or we can accept what the future promises: a universal radioactive waste-land where the survivors will envy the dead." He bowed formally. "Thank you."

The crowd vigorously applauded, rising from their folding chairs. Osato bowed again and stepped from the platform. He approached the fellow members of *Anzen Sekai*.

"Congratulations, Osato-san," Sakata Fujo said in their native language. A big man by Japanese standards, Sakata was a superb physical specimen, conditioned by years of karate training that earned him a sixth-dan black belt. His only flaw was the blind, milky-white left eye he was born with. "The Americans are moved by your speech."

"*Hai,*" Osato replied softly. "Yes. The flames of protest have been lit. When the next accident occurs, fuel will ignite that fire into a righteous blaze that will consume the American nuclear program forever."

"And that time will come soon," Sakata said firm-ly, a smile raising the ends of his long mustache.

"*Hai,*" Osato confirmed with a confident nod.

4

Osato Goro and his followers were unaware a special team of men threatened their plan. As the antinuke demonstrators cheered Goro, David McCarter and Keio Ohara stood inside the compound area of the Quinton plant.

"Quite a cheerleader, isn't he?" David commented dryly.

"There is truth in what he says," K.O. replied in a flat voice.

"I wouldn't have guessed you'd be opposed to nuclear energy," the Englishman said. "You've always seemed like a rather modern-thinking Oriental."

"I'm also a post-World War II Japanese," K.O. said. "We are *very* familiar with what atom bombs did at Hiroshima and Nagasaki. Don't misunderstand my stance on this subject. There is some truth in what Osato Goro says. But I do not totally agree with him."

"I should hope not," David said, tugging at the lapel of his rumpled sport jacket, which concealed a

Browning 9mm automatic in a shoulder-holster rig. "After all, that fella thinks the whole bleeding world will ban nuclear research because he wants them to feel guilty. If Western Europe, the United States and the rest of the free world agree to that, then what happens? *All* nuclear power will be in the hands of the iron-curtain countries, that's what."

"Quite so," the Japanese agreed. "But because one is not opposed to something does not mean it should be free of criticism. There have been serious errors in the construction of nuclear plants and poor judgment in the sites chosen for such installations. Osato-san might exaggerate, but these facts should not be ignored."

"Well, we're not dealing with maintenance failure or human error here," McCarter snorted. "Bloody saboteurs tried to cause that accident two days earlier."

K.O. nodded grimly. "Very unusual saboteurs."

The pair strolled to the north wall and examined the high wire fence. The Englishman shook his head.

"I don't see how they scaled the bugger without setting off the alarms," he admitted. "The controls in the guard tower were shut off when the bastards left, but how'd they get over the fence in the first place?"

"They did not touch it," K.O. replied.

"What the hell?" The Briton glared at his companion. "Are you telling me they flew over that thing in a hang glider or something?"

"No," the Oriental answered. "One of them jumped over it."

"Jumped!" David retorted. "That's ridiculous. That fence is twenty feet high. Nobody could—"

"The others served as a springboard for their accomplice," K.O. explained. "Like a troop of acrobats, they formed a human staircase and their comrade hurled himself over the top."

"And dropped twenty feet to the concrete?" The Briton snorted. "That's a good way to break a leg."

"He knew how to land and roll with the fall."

"How did he avoid activating those?" David asked, pointing at the pavement. Wires were installed in the cracks, acting as sensors to detect body heat and movement. There were also electrical eyes built into the walls, equally sensitive to intruders. "You're the electrical wizard, K.O. How'd they get in without setting those off?"

"I don't know," the Japanese admitted with a modest shrug.

"At least that answer makes sense," McCarter said, rolling his eyes in frustration. "Any bright ideas on how the other terrorists got over the fence?"

"The man chosen for the task climbed the guard tower and deactivated the fence's alarm system."

"The only door leading to the stairs was locked. How'd he manage to scale the tower? It's as smooth as a baby's arse. Is he a human fly as well as a bloody jumping jack?''

"Correct," K.O. answered simply.

The Japanese walked to the tower. David cursed under his breath, struggling to keep up with K.O.'s long strides. K.O. touched the tower's wall and grimly nodded at the deep scratches in the surface.

"There is your answer," he declared. "The terrorist wore *tekagi* to claw into the concrete, creating his own hand and foot holds where none existed."

"*Tea-ka-gee?*" The Englishman was more confused than ever.

"*Tekagi,*" K.O. confirmed. "Sometimes called tiger claws. Metal claws strapped to the hands and feet. They serve as either scaling devices or weapons."

"The guard's throat had been ripped open," David recalled. "You know something, don't you? What are you hiding from the rest of us, damn it?" The Englishman's short temper was beginning to boil.

"I had to be certain before I voiced my suspicions," K.O. calmly told him. "Now they are confirmed."

"What the hell kind of men are we dealing with, K.O.?" McCarter demanded.

"Ninja," his companion answered.

A sudden chill caused the Briton to gather his jacket together. The chill had nothing to do with the weather.

Gary Manning grunted as he, Rafael and Yak followed the propeller-mouthed assistant manager across the compound of the Wadsworth Nuclear Power Plant, located along the Des Moines River in Iowa. The fence surrounding the installation was only twelve feet high and had no alarm systems. Television cameras monitored the barrier and the grounds within, but there were no secondary alarms or sensors. The security was far less than that at Quinton. The Canadian wondered how many other nuclear installations were as vulnerable to terrorism.

A hard-nosed businessman, Gary recognized the value of atomic energy. His expertise with demolitions also made him indifferent to the fact that a reactor core contains great explosive potential. Yet the Canadian was horrified by the consequences of a full-scale meltdown. The possibility of widespread radioactive contamination threatened to be disastrous to the environment. A woodsman, Gary recoiled at the thought of the impact a serious nuclear accident would have on nature.

"As you can see," Mr. Ballard, the round-faced manager said with a professional smile, "we operate three turbogenerators twenty-four hours a day." He gestured toward the three monster silos forming a huge horseshoe around the white reactor globe. "We've never had a malfunction or accident. Our personnel are highly trained professionals, and the equipment is kept in excellent condition."

"And the security stinks," Gary muttered under his breath.

Rafael yawned. When he wasn't teamed with Phoenix Force, he worked as an insurance investigator specializing in maritime claims. His occupation brought him in constant contact with chatterboxes like Ballard, and they never failed to bore him.

Yakov scratched his right arm above the elbow. He wore a tweed jacket inappropriate for summer weather. The sleeve was filled with an ingenious prosthetic device attached to his abbreviated limb. Only the stiffness of the velvet-gloved fingers of his right hand suggested it wasn't made of flesh and bone.

They approached the squat office building located beside the reactor dome. Yak raised his heavy eyebrows with surprise. "You must not have much of a staff here," he remarked.

"Most of the plant is automated," Ballard declared proudly. "But we have a full crew of twenty-two excellent technicians on duty around the clock."

"How many security personnel?" Gary asked bluntly.

"Well—" the assistant manager shrugged "—four or five guards."

"The Havana gambling casinos had better security in Batista's day," Rafael said, toying with the red-

and-yellow NRC pass badge pinned to the lapel of his navy blue blazer.

"Just follow me," Ballard urged. "Everything is run from this little building. That's efficiency!"

"That's an easy target," the Canadian said, rolling his eyes. A quarter pound of C-4 could blow the whole structure apart—including the equipment that operates the control rods within the reactor, the coolant system and the water pumps.

A red-faced security guard recognized the assistant manager and pressed the button to open an electrically powered door. At least the glass looked shatterproof, Gary noticed. A number of closed-circuit television sets on the guard's office wall monitored the fence on all sides. Ballard smiled broadly and gestured at the surveillance system.

"As you can see," he declared, "we have a fine security operation."

"Just like a department store," Rafael muttered.

"Bob called from the gate, sir," the chunky guard said. "He told me these gentlemen are carrying firearms."

"They're part of a security inspection team from the Justice Department, with special authorization from the Nuclear Regulatory Commission, Paul. It's okay."

"By the way, the camera on the west side is on the fritz, sir," Paul told Ballard. "I've called maintenance to check it out."

"Haven't you sent anyone to secure the area?" Yak asked the guard.

"Really, Mr. Goldberg," the manager said, addressing the Israeli by his cover name. "It's three o'clock in the afternoon. Security is one thing. Paranoia is another."

"There's no such thing as being too careful when you're dealing with enough fissionable material to roast the entire state of Iowa," Gary stated flatly.

"Of course," Ballard said. "Paul, see to it we get a man out there immediately."

"Yes, sir." The guard nodded.

"Now, er . . . let me show you the control room."

The manager led the three Phoenix Force men down a short corridor to a thick steel door. He removed a flat metal key from his pocket and inserted it into a slot by the door.

"It's computer operated," Ballard smiled. "This key triggers a microphone built into the memory banks. The door won't open unless the speaker's voiceprint is filed in the computer."

"Open sesame," Rafael remarked dryly.

"Darrell C. Ballard," the assistant manager announced. "Authorization code blue."

The door slowly hummed open.

Ballard turned to Gary. "See?"

The thud of bullets striking flesh was almost as loud as the phut-phut of the silenced pistol. Ballard stumbled backward from the impact of the slugs, an expression of astonishment pasted on his face. The assistant manager toppled to the linoleum. Blood stained the breast pocket of his suit.

"Cristo," Rafael whispered, jumping clear of the doorway. Yak and Gary followed his example.

They glanced into the next room and saw the control panels, computers and other equipment within. Several white-smocked figures lay on the immaculate tile floor. A man dressed in black held a pistol in both hands and fired two more muffled shots, while his comrades scrambled to assist him.

The Phoenix men could only guess how many opponents lurked in the control room, but their intentions were obvious.

To disable the automated Wadsworth plant would require little more than pulling a plug or two. Then the countdown to a runaway reactor meltdown would begin. Phoenix Force couldn't spare a moment in planning the action. Rafael responded first. Bending to draw a compact Walther PPK from an ankle holster, he dove into the control room.

The enemy gunman's weapon coughed again as the Cuban hurtled over the threshold. A .380 bullet burned air above Rafael. He hit the floor in a fast shoulder roll and came up on one knee, pistol held in a two-handed Weaver's grip. The Walther barked twice. His gasp muffled by the black scarf across his nose and mouth, the black-garbed figure convulsed as two .32-caliber dumdum slugs bit into his chest. The gunman collapsed.

Other shadowy figures darted about the room, hastily selecting cover among the computers, panels and other machines. Rafael snapped off two shots as he dashed to the shelter of a stout galvanometer. Gary Manning unsheathed a Colt Python from a shoulder holster and burst into the room.

One of the black-clad terrorists hurled a star-shaped object at the Canadian. The projectile struck the doorway and fell harmlessly to the floor. The Python boomed in response, the recoil of the big revolver carrying Gary's arm toward the ceiling. A 158-grain .357 hollowpoint slug crashed into the center of the would-be assassin's chest. The force of the Magnum bullet kicked the terrorist across the room. He fell in a lifeless heap beside a computer-printout machine.

Cursing himself for not bringing a gun, Yak charged into the room. Two terrorists, crouched at the corner of the main control panel for the reactor rods and coolant system, opened fire with silenced automatics. Luckily the sound suppressors reduced accuracy, and the bullets pelted the yellow tile wall behind the Israeli. Yak joined Gary at the cover of a computer processor, while Rafael sent two quick Walther rounds at the gunmen.

A terrorist screamed, dropped his H&K automatic and clawed at his bullet-torn shoulder. The other hooded killer swung his Browning pocket pistol toward the Cuban. Gary's Python roared, echoing within the room like an exploding furnace in the caverns of hell. The terrorist's head burst open from the .357 round. Brains, blood and skull fragments splattered against the yellow tile wall.

Rafael moved cautiously forward, hoping to capture the wounded invader before the man could reclaim his weapon. A blur of movement at the corner of his eye caused the Cuban to whirl. Yet another black-clad killer was lurking on the opposite side of the galvanometer! The man threw an odd, three-pronged steel weapon at Rafael's head. Its long center blade missed the intended target but slapped Rafael's forearm hard. The PPK fell from the Cuban's numb fingers.

The terrorist screamed, thrusting the point of his weapon at Rafael's midsection.

Trained in *shito-ryu* karate, the Cuban recognized his opponent's instrument—a *sai*. The three-pronged device was originally a farm tool, until Okinawan martial artists learned to employ it as a weapon against sword-wielding bandits. Rafael had seen demonstrations of *sai* techniques in *dojos*, but the instruments—unlike his adversary's—had blunted tips. He was so stunned to find himself being attacked by such an unlikely and impractical weapon he almost failed to move in time to avoid the killer's lunge.

He stepped aside, and the *sai* stabbed air. Rafael quickly seized the terrorist's wrist with his right hand and thrust his left elbow into the man's armpit. The killer hissed through his mask as Rafael jerked the captive limb down hard, simultaneously applying pressure to the nerve center under his arm. The *sai* clattered to the floor.

With a *kiai* shout the terrorist punted a foot into the back of Rafael's knee. The Cuban's leg buckled, and his opponent wrenched free of the hold. A vicious back fist to the face knocked Rafael to his knees. He tasted blood, but reacted automatically and reached to the small of his back with his right hand.

The killer lashed a black-booted foot at Rafael's head, aiming for the vulnerable left temple. Rafael's left forearm connected with his assailant's calf, blocking the kick as he drew the knife from its sheath. He plunged the five-inch, double-edged blade into the terrorist's solar plexus. The point penetrated upward, entering the heart in a single thrust.

Despite the agony of a broken collarbone, the terrorist with a .32 bullet in his shoulder had gathered his H&K 9mm pistol and continued to fire at Gary and Yak. The Canadian's revolver snarled in reply. A powerful .357 slug split the aluminum rim of the control panel. The shadowy invader ducked down quickly.

"Damn," Gary muttered. "If I'd had my deer rifle, I would have nailed that son of a bitch."

"Just keep him pinned down," Yak urged.

The Canadian nodded and squeezed off another shot while the senior member of Phoenix Force moved from the shelter of the computer processor. Yak shuffled across the floor rapidly for a man his age and size, his body huddled so low his left hand slapped the tiles. His prosthetic arm was held forward like the lance of a charging knight. The Israeli reached the main control panel. He took a deep breath and mentally said a brief prayer before he threw himself to the floor.

Yak landed on his side, purposely propelling himself with enough force to slide along the length of the panel. The startled terrorist glanced down and saw the Israeli lying a few feet away, right "hand" pointed at him, the left bracing the prosthetic wrist.

The killer pivoted and swung his H&K toward the unexpected threat. A sharp crack accompanied a ribbon of yellow flame, and the velvet cloth at the gloved tip of Yak's right index "finger" burst apart. The .22 Magnum bullet struck the terrorist between the scarf and hood, puncturing the bridge of his nose, sizzling into his brain. He died with an expression of total amazement frozen in his dark Oriental eyes.

"That's all of them," Rafael announced, his knife in one hand and the Walther PPK in the other.

"Yeah," Gary agreed as he shook the spent cartridges from his revolver and began to reload. "But what the hell were they? I never saw terrorists like these before."

"I suspect K.O. can give us some answers," Yak said. He removed the glove from his right "hand," revealing the artificial extremity of steel, bolts and cables. The index "finger" featured a machined hole at its end—the barrel and muzzle of the .22 Magnum pistol built into the prosthetic device. "At least I hope so," he added.

5

Sakata Fujo made sharp *kiai* shouts as he executed a flawless series of *katas*, the dancelike patterns used in karate. Dressed in a *gi*—martial arts uniform—he became a white blur bisected by the black belt around his middle. His arms and legs moved rapidly but smoothly; his hands and feet struck out at invisible opponents.

The martial artist completed his *kata* routine and turned to the spectators seated in the gymnasium in Omaha, Nebraska. He bowed formally as subdued applause acknowledged the first part of his demonstration. Most of the people in the audience were Americans who didn't find punching and kicking thin air terribly impressive.

Sakata gestured to four smaller young Japanese, also clad in *gi* uniforms, with less prestigious brown belts. The foursome approached the mat, each carrying two thick squares of pinewood. The audience watched silently as the four brown belts formed a circle around Sakata. They held the boards at chest level, arms extended stiffly. Sakata breathed deeply and slowly lowered a fist to his hip.

"Haaii-yaa!" he cried as he drove a *seiken* punch into the closest target.

Two pinewood sections, each four inches thick, cracked from the force of the blow. Sakata whirled and slashed the side of his hand into another pair of boards, breaking them with equal ease. He swiftly moved to one side and thrust the edge of his right foot into a third target, shattering wood once more. Finally he stepped close to the last man and slammed the point of his elbow into the remaining boards. Four splintered parts fell to the mat. The audience responded with vigorous applause.

Osato Goro smiled as he watched the admiration on the onlookers' faces. Typical Americans, he thought. They fail to appreciate the grace, timing and proper technique of a kata, but they admire raw power. Strength was all they respected; destruction impressed them. So be it.

A man rose from the bleachers and strolled casually from the gymnasium while Sakata Fujo and his assistants prepared another karate exhibition. Stepping into a dimly lit corridor, Osato removed a pack of smokes from his pocket. He never smoked in front of the antinuke crowds. The idiots expected their leaders to be pure in all things. "How can you be concerned about the environment, yet purposely pollute your own lungs?" they asked. Osato realized the importance of presenting a proper image.

"American cigarettes are one of the best things about this country, eh?" someone said from the shadows.

The speaker stepped forward. A medium-built man in his forties with a belly and a receding hairline, he did not stand out in a crowd. Dressed in a polo shirt and Bermuda shorts, he resembled a vacationing laborer. A cheap pair of sunglasses added to his average appearance.

"What we'll accomplish makes being in this country worthwhile, Major," Osato replied flatly, taking a cigarette from the pack.

"I wish you wouldn't address me by rank," the other man said, speaking fluent English with an American accent. "I'm known as Donald Grover."

"I am aware of that," the Japanese assured him. He lit the smoke. "How do you like Fujo's demonstration? He's a sixth-dan black belt, you know."

"Impressive," Grover snorted. "I told you on the phone I didn't care for your choice of meeting places, and I don't think your second-in-command should be showing off his karate tricks in public. *Anzen Sekai* is an organization of pacifists. Sakata is hardly maintaining that image."

Osato smiled. "Americans expect Orientals to be martial artists. Most practitioners of these arts endorse a philosophy of nonviolence unless forced to use their skills in self-defense. Sakata is familiar with this since his instructors taught such nonsense. He will tell the audience the proper things. I did not make him my lieutenant merely because he is an expert at hand-to-hand combat. Fujo is a shrewd intelligent man. Have no fear of that.''

''I hope you're right,'' Grover remarked. ''You claim your Tigers of Justice have been trained for more than two years for the assignment we've undertaken. They're supposed to be experts with explosives, firearms and that *ninjutsu* martial art that's supposed to turn men into supercommandos. That's why my superiors at the Kremlin agreed to your scheme.''

''A halt to nuclear research in the United States would be most desirable to the Soviet Union, yes?''

''The KGB wouldn't have called me into action if there wasn't enormous potential in this operation. I've been in this country for fifteen years, and I've managed to get a federal-government position that has one hell of a security clearance. I've waited a long time to get my orders from Moscow for this one special mission.''

''And now it has arrived,'' the Japanese stated.

''Yeah,'' Grover muttered. ''But I'm not terribly impressed by the results so far.''

Osato Goro's expression remained blank. ''The sabotage of the plant in Indiana failed because *you* did not tell us we were dealing with a heavy-water reactor. We must receive proper information for future assignments," he said. "Anyway, the attempt was still a partial success. Although a meltdown did not occur, the public is outraged by the accident. I trust you heard about this."

"You gave a very nice speech," Grover admitted. "Your ability to influence others is one of your greatest talents. True, the incident at the Quinton plant has caused more protests about nuclear power—thanks to the government's decision to conceal the truth. Washington obviously feels the public will be less alarmed if they believe a malfunction occurred instead of attempted sabotage and murder."

"Killing an enemy in war is not murder," Osato said stiffly. "The Americans are my enemies—especially those who willingly form an allegiance with supporters of nuclear energy. We are at war with them and their insidious power-mad plans!"

"Forgive me," Grover urged. "I used a poor choice of words."

The Soviet sleeper agent had been trained to handle fanatics like Osato Goro. Indeed, the KGB—and all intelligence organizations—utilize radicals of every political, religious and emotional extreme. Such individuals are fiercely dedicated to their particular cause. Their obsessions drive them to take risks professional clandestine operators would not consider.

Fanatics are useful, but they must be handled properly. Regardless of their ideology, zealots are emotional, potentially volatile. Most are mentally unbalanced and paranoid, distrusting anyone with a philosophy other than their own. A radical, therefore, can change from an asset to a liability if he becomes suspicious of an ally.

"It does not matter," the Japanese said. "The plant in Iowa is an easy target for my men. Even if they try to improve security, no one will expect us to strike in broad daylight." Osato smiled. "Even as we speak, the worst nuclear 'accident' of all time is taking place. A total reactor meltdown that will spill death and radioactive fallout for hundreds of miles. It will cripple the Americans' nuclear program—if it doesn't bring it to a total halt. This is what both the KGB and my Tigers of Justice want, yes?"

Grover managed to conceal his disgust. *The Tigers of Justice!* Osato had selected thirty-seven Japanese fanatics and formed the vengeful terrorist cult. Like their leader, they hated Americans because they dropped two atomic bombs at the end of World War II. Most were from Hiroshima and Nagasaki. They either bore a birth defect or had close relatives who were crippled or mutilated by the effects of radiation on their genes—although mercury poisoning in fish consumed by mothers may have been responsible in many cases. Using *Anzen Sekai* as a cover for the cult, Osato created an organization of fearless, well-trained commandos who were dedicated to the destruction of nuclear power and willing to go to any lengths to accomplish their goal.

The Tigers of Justice were not Communists. Their obsession was not based on politics. Most despised the Soviet Union for dabbling in atomic energy and weapons. They would not have approved of Osato Goro's arrangement with the KGB. Only Osato and his lieutenant, Sakata Fujo, knew the true source of their organization's financing and support.

"Well, I've got some bad news for you, my friend," Grover began, controlling his voice to avoid revealing his frustration and anger. "My contacts in Iowa have already informed me that your sabotage attempt failed."

Osato looked at the KGB man sharply. "Do they know what went wrong?"

"Not yet," Grover sighed. "But if the meltdown had been successful, there would be efforts to evacuate the surrounding areas."

"Perhaps not," Osato stated, but he puffed nervously on his smoke. "My men may have been delayed."

"They may have been captured," the Soviet spy replied. His hands sunk into the pockets of his shorts. "How much do they know?"

"They probably decided to cancel the mission," the Japanese assured him. "Besides, they would never be taken alive."

"They'd better not be," Grover warned. "If the authorities learn you're involved, they might find out about me, too."

"You needn't worry about my men," Osato insisted. "Each Tiger ninja carries a capsule of nicotine sulfate. They'll use it if they must."

"I thought hara-kiri went out of fashion after World War II."

"The correct term for ritual suicide by disembowelment is seppuku," the Japanese said. "And I know my men. They are as willing to sacrifice their lives as I am."

Grover smiled. "Let's hope it doesn't come to that. You'd better prepare for your next target."

"It will be the plant in Kansas," Osato announced.

"The Hamel installation?" Grover's eyebrows rose. "I thought we agreed that one is too dangerous. I couldn't find any weakness in its security. Besides, it's a breeder reactor, for Christ sake!"

"You have been in America a long time." The Oriental smiled. "What would your superiors in the Kremlin think if they discovered one of their comrades gave up Marxism for Christianity?"

Grover ignored the barb. "A breeder produces plutonium. Nobody can predict what that stuff might do in the case of a meltdown."

"So?" Osato shrugged. "I care no more about the lives of Americans than they did for the Japanese when they dropped the atom bomb on Hiroshima."

"Forget Hamel," Grover demanded. He gripped the specially designed pushtop cigarette lighter in his pocket. It was actually a weapon that fired tiny steel darts no thicker than the lead in a pencil. Dipped in a synthetic poison similar to cyanide, the projectiles cause death within seconds. If Osato's obsession had driven him mad, the KGB man would kill him—silently and quickly.

"Listen to my plan, Major," the Japanese stated calmly.

"There's no way to penetrate the plant's security, and anybody you send would have to be crazy," Grover growled. "Your men aren't kamikazes, damn it!"

"No," Osato agreed. "But you've almost guessed how we're going to deal with the Hamel installation."

Grover relaxed his grip on the lighter. "I'm listening," he said.

6

"The origins of the ninja is clouded in mystery," Keio Ohara said to his fellow Phoenix Force members and Wade Sommer, Milton Cohen and Harrison Reed. "However, most believe it began in twelfth-century Japan...."

"What has this got to do with the sabotage attempts on nuclear plants?" Reed demanded.

"If you'll shut up, you'll find out," David McCarter said sharply.

The NRC man glared at McCarter but didn't speak. Sommer seemed embarrassed by the Englishman's bluntness. Cohen smiled thinly, and Rafael chuckled aloud.

After learning of the incident at the Wadsworth plant, K.O. and David caught the first plane to Iowa. The Justice Department and Nuclear Regulatory Commission were also contacted. The eight men congregated at the Indianapolis Hilton, where Yak, Rafael and Gary were staying. They'd rented the hotel's smallest conference room to discuss the terrorist situation.

"The ninja were espionage agents and assassins in feudal Japan," K.O. continued, wishing his knowledge of Oriental history and martial arts hadn't burdened him with having to deliver a lecture. "There was great turmoil in those days. Political and social intrigue were common. *Daimyos*—'warlords'—schemed to acquire greater power, and many plots involved clandestine operations. The ninja were called in for such tasks."

"In other words, they were hired killers?" Sommer inquired.

K.O. shook his head. "They were far more than that. True, ninja were trained in many methods of murder. They studied virtually all martial arts. They were taught to kill with bare hands, sword, bow and arrow, spear, *shuriken* and other weapons. The ninja utilized explosives and firearms long before the samurai would accept such 'modern' notions. Yet assassination was seldom their primary goal. Roughly translated, *ninjutsu* means 'the art of stealth' or 'invisibility.' This is not as absurd as it may sound. Ninja agents were taught to camouflage themselves and to move with the silence of a cat.

"Most ninja assignments were reconnaissance missions. The ninja were trained accordingly and taught to deal with any situation or environment. They were adept at scaling walls and even walking on ceilings. Ninja were expert watermen, woodsmen and mountain climbers. They also learned to impersonate beggers, merchants, priests and samurai.''

"Combination commando and espionage agent,'' Yak mused, lighting a cigarette with a battered lighter. "Fascinating.''

"How did one become a ninja?'' Gary asked. "I don't imagine they put an ad in the paper: 'Help Wanted—Need Oriental superman for impossible missions. Weaklings and retards need not apply.'''

K.O. grinned. "Feudal Japan was a very class-oriented society. One's position in life generally depended upon birth. The ninja were no exception. They were products of the lower class. Born to ninja parents in a ninja clan, they began training as soon as they were able to walk. The ninja chain of command consisted of the *jonin*—leaders; *chunin*—subchiefs; and *genin*, or field agents.''

"Forgive me, Mr. Tanaka,'' Milton Cohen said, addressing K.O. by his alias. "But I find it difficult to believe someone has hired a clan of these ninjas to sabotage our nuclear power plants.''

"Not genuine ninja agents,'' the Japanese agreed. "If such clans still exist, their activities are probably restricted to the Orient. However, the terrorists we're dealing with have clearly been trained in a form of *ninjutsu*. If the *shuriken*—spike—and *tekagi*—tiger claws—used at the Quinton plant are not enough, we certainly have ample proof after the incident at the Wadsworth installation.''

"Yeah," Gary Manning remarked as he tossed a six-pointed metal object on the table. "One of them threw this at me."

"That star-shaped thing is a weapon?" Reed inquired.

"It is a *shaken*," K.O. explained. "Another device used in *shuriken-jutsu*, a martial art employing hand-thrown projectiles."

"Another bastard tried to run me through with this," Rafael declared, holding up the *sai*.

"Nearly had a fishkabob, eh?" David joked.

Rafael smiled.

"We found no identification on the bodies," Yak stated. "Fingerprints and dental records might reveal something, but don't count on it. We can also try to trace the serial numbers on their weapons—although it's probably a waste of time. Terrorists don't buy firearms from legitimate gun shops, and black-market dealers don't keep records."

"But we did find one clue," Gary declared. He placed a black cloth the size of a handkerchief on the table. "One of the terrorists had this in his pocket."

The emblem of a yellow tiger with an open mouth dominated the center of the cloth. Red ideograms decorated both sides of the cat.

"Does this mean anything to you?" Sommer asked Keio Ohara.

"It's Japanese," K.O. replied. "It says, 'Tigers of Justice.'"

"What the hell does that mean?" Reed demanded.

"It means the terrorists are Japanese," Sommer stated. "Yet, you don't think these are real ninja killers, Mr. Tanaka?"

K.O. nodded. "This banner suggests we are dealing with fanatics, not true espionage agents."

"The primary terrorist organization in Japan is the Red Army," Yak remarked. "Maybe this is an extremist branch of it. The Tigers of Justice could even be a renegade group like Al Fatah. Even the PLO doesn't want to be associated with the vermin in Black September."

"The Red Army has never conducted operations in this country," K.O. replied. "Some of their members have teamed up with Arab or Latin Communist groups, but they lack the finances or contacts to conduct missions in the United States. The North Koreans and occasionally the Chinese are their main supporters. I doubt Peking would endorse this kind of terrorism."

"Of course not," David snorted. "The bloody U.S. government plans to sell the Commie chinks weapons! Brilliant policies you Yanks have!"

"Let's not discuss politics," Rafael urged. He had refereed enough arguments between Phoenix Force members to see one coming. Yak and Gary were somewhat left of center, while K.O. and David were to the right. After suffering torture in Castro's prison and betrayal by the U.S. during the Bay of

Pigs, the Cuban had become the ultimate political cynic.

"If they aren't from the Red Army, maybe they're some sort of military right-wing group," Gary suggested. "They might be trying to get America to sever relations with Japan so Nippon can return to the 'way of the samurai' and become an isolationist country once more."

"If they were trying to blackmail the United States into changing its policies, they'd be making demands by now." Yak sighed. "I suspect we're dealing with a bizarre new organization of some kind."

"Not totally new," Professor Cohen mused. "Since they use tactics of the ninja, we should have some idea what to expect from them."

"Ninja techniques varied considerably," K.O. replied. "They were master escape artists, able to dislocate joints in order to free themselves from bonds. They trained dogs and monkeys to attack pursuers. Ninja were skilled pharmacists, capable of making gunpowder, poisons and other chemicals. They devised a solution that made crickets and frogs unable to stop chirping. Thus their silence would not betray the presence of a ninja.

"Some were brilliant strategists. *Daimyo*—warlords—occasionally put *jonin*—chiefs—in charge of high-born samurai in battle. Ninja even attempted aerial assaults, using winged gliding devices and kites large enough to support a man. However, such tactics were seldom successful. One trick consisted of flying kites with ninja dummies attached. The enemy forces would be distracted by the 'flying invaders' while the real assault team entered the stronghold from another position.''

"It sounds as if these ninja understood the philosophy of terrorism,'' Gary commented.

"They did.'' K.O. nodded. "The ninja invented the 'dragon ship,' a boat disguised as a sea monster. Some wore masks of demons or spirits to frighten superstitious opponents. And they used magic. . . .''

"What?'' Reed said. "This is utter nonsense!''

"The magic I speak of is sleight of hand,'' the Japanese explained. "Ninja would walk on water using flotation devices on their feet. They carried trained mice and weasels. When pursued, the agent would release the animal and hide in a tree. Thus many believed a ninja could transform himself into another creature. Ninja used blinding powders and smoke bombs to help them 'disappear' like a magician. Once a ninja who was surrounded by enemies committed seppuku with a knife. When his opponents saw the blood pour from his abdomen, they turned away. The ninja suddenly rose from the ground and fled. He had actually cut open a rabbit hidden under his clothing.''

"Didn't the ninja use some type of hypnotism?'' Rafael inquired.

"Yes,'' the Japanese confirmed. "It was called *sai-*

min jutsu and consisted of moving one's fingers in a special serpentine manner to mesmerize opponents. It was part of the ninja's mystical practice of *kuji-kiri*.''

"This is all very interesting," Sommer said, "but how'd these ninjas—or whatever they are—mesmerize their way into those nuclear power plants? None of this explains how they just walked through electric eyes and sensors without activating the alarms.''

"If we can capture one of the bastards, maybe we can get a few answers," David suggested.

"I doubt it," K.O. replied. "The ninja were rarely taken alive because they faced execution by slow and horrible means. They'd sooner take their own lives by sword or knife. More than one ninja bit off his own tongue and bled to death. They were also fiercely loyal to their clans. Ninja often slashed their faces and disfigured themselves to prevent their enemies from tracing them to their headquarters.''

"Barbaric," Reed muttered, shaking his head.

"It was their culture," K.O. stated. "To the ninja, it was a way of life.''

"If these Tigers of Justice are modern-day ninja agents," Gary Manning began, "they've added silenced pistols and plastique to their traditional arsenal.''

"Not to mention some sort of technical wizardry

that allows them to penetrate the most sophisticated electronic surveillance devices," Yak added.

"At least now we have some idea about what sort of adversaries we're up against," Rafael mused. "Although I liked it better when we didn't!"

7

Lonny Cox glanced from the blur of the propeller at the nose of his Stearman to the instrument panel. He recalled he'd once considered flying to be the greatest pleasure a man could have without a waterbed. To operate his own airplane, to actually make a living by sailing a mile high, had been his dream. Lonny worked overtime at manual labor, made do with patched furniture and a weary old Ford and sacrificed his social life to save enough money to meet his goal. He met it. And now he was sick to death of it.

Flying had become a tedious routine. Each day Lonny dragged his ass out of bed before dawn, checked his schedule while consuming black coffee and cigarettes and then started up the cantankerous Stearman. Then he'd fly over the vast green fields of Kansas until he located the farm that needed its crops dusted with insecticides.

When he wasn't dumping clouds of chemicals, he sold rides to bumpkins who'd never been in an airplane. Occasionally he ran deliveries for small businesses that wanted something taken or picked up in another part of the state. He worked his butt off and barely made ends meet.

In the winter he didn't dare take his old Stearman off the ground. He struggled, working as an assistant mechanic. Put it together and he was still barely earning enough income to keep body, soul and aircraft together. Then he had the additional headaches of the goddamn bureaucrats. The Federal Aviation Administration constantly wanted to know what condition his plane was in and bitched if he didn't check his spark plugs every ninety days. The Environmental Protection Agency inspected the kind of poisons he used and how much he released into the atmosphere, as if he could single-handedly destroy the ozone layer. Also, the infernal Internal Revenue Service made certain he didn't pocket any undeclared income before they claimed half of it.

The engine of the Stearman growled as Lonny looked through the window and grimaced at the familiar scene below: a dirt runway, a run-down house with a leaky roof and an old barn he'd converted into a hangar. Home sweet home. How the hell had he ever been stupid enough to think being a self-employed sky jockey would be a carefree life of fun and profit? Jesus, he'd got himself into a mess and there didn't seem to be any way out of it.

Reducing the throttle, he aimed the Stearman at the runway. Lonny pulled the stick back, raising the nose of the craft slightly as the plane neared the ground. The wheels touched down. Lonny felt the familiar jar of the mild impact and stopped the power. The plane rolled three hundred feet before the pilot killed the engine.

"Screw you, you mechanical bastard," Lonny muttered, climbing out of the cockpit.

He stepped onto the wing and hopped down, grateful to have the earth under his feet. His nostrils were filled with dust and the stink of insecticide. The job was probably fouling up his lungs like a three-pack-a-day habit. He glanced at his watch and cursed. Two fifty-three. Crap. Lonny was scheduled to dust old man Fenton's crops at four.

Lonny headed for the house, eager to wash the grit from his face and rinse similar crud down his throat with a cold beer or two. He almost hoped his rusty old refrigerator had conked out; that would give him an excuse to drive into Beloit and spend the rest of the day in a nice cool tavern.

Opening the screen door, he wondered if he could sell the place to some dumb-ass dreamer who still thought it would be great to buzz around in the clouds all day. Then he could try to become a full-time mechanic. It's a crummy way to make a living, Lonny thought, stepping across the threshold into the kitchen, but there are no good ways. . . .

Suddenly something grabbed him from behind. Lonny seldom locked his doors in the daytime. Who'd rip him off out in the boonies? The bastard that had an arm wrapped around his neck, that's who! Lonny clawed at the strong forearm that threatened to close off his windpipe as the assailant's other hand moved under the pilot's armpit, clasping a palm to the back of his head.

In desperation he tried to ram an elbow into his attacker's ribs. Then the killer slammed a knee into the small of Lonny's back. His feet slid out from under him, weight swinging forward while the viselike grip held his head stationary. Vertebra cracked. Lonny Cox crumpled to the floor.

"Yoi shigoto, Nasaki," a young, flat-faced Oriental said, limping from another room. "Good work, Nasaki."

"Domo, Hirito." The assassin bowed curtly. "Thank you, Hirito." Slightly larger than his companion, Nasaki's otherwise handsome face was marred by a harelip—an affliction he blamed on an atomic explosion at Hiroshima almost a decade before he was born.

"Let us hope the rest of our mission proves as successful," Hirito said. His foot dragged as he shuffled forward. He also considered his physical disability to be the fault of the bomb—and the United States of America.

"The task is a simple one," Nasaki commented. "Perhaps too simple."

"The less complicated a plan, the less can go wrong, yes?"

Both men wore denim slacks and checkered shirts. Their assignment did not require the black ninja garments employed by fellow Tigers of Justice on previous missions. The only unusual item of clothing was Nasaki's paratrooper boots. Hirito helped his comrade slip into the shoulder harness of a bulky backpack. Nasaki buckled a belt around his waist and checked the metal ring at his rib cage.

"I wish I could go with you," Hirito said sadly, looking at his clubfoot with resentment.

"Your part in the plan is as important as mine, my brother," Nasaki replied.

"Perhaps." The crippled man sighed. "May great fortune travel with you, my brother."

"*Domo*, Hirito. *Domo*."

Nasaki rolled the Stearman along the runway. He had flown similar planes in the Japanese Air Corps with little difficulty. The corpse of Lonny Cox wiggled in the passenger's seat, the head rolling loosely on its broken neck. Hirito, envious of his partner, watched the plane rise from the ground. Nasaki had been given the dangerous assignment—he would strike a great blow against the American nuclear power establishment and possibly achieve a glorious death in the process. Hirito cursed his maimed limb for denying him this honor. Yet, as he limped to the battered blue Volkswagen they'd stolen from the parking lot of a Beloit shopping center that morning, Hirito found some comfort in one thought: before

the day ended, both of them might get to die for their
cause.

The Stearman flew over miles of farmland, its cross-
shaped shadow creeping across the ground like a
black vulture. Nasaki grimly stared through his gog-
gles. Born in a country that had suffered for cen-
turies from overpopulation, he hated the United
States for its abundance of land and uncrowded
space. Why had this nation's karma—destiny—
granted its people so much? Americans had better
food, clothing, medical care and more privileges than
any other people. Yet they were a ruthless race with a
vicious technology. They deserved the devastation
the Tigers of Justice were about to unleash on their
land—a land that had not been scarred by war since
the barbarians fought in a bloody civil conflict more
than a hundred years before.

Nasaki smiled when he saw his target in the distance. The giant smokestacks of turbogenerators
positioned on each side of the reactor dome reminded
the Japanese terrorist of a horned demon poking its
head through the ground. It was a devil with its own
uranium hell locked within. In a few minutes Nasaki
would unleash that ungodly fury upon the nation he
despised so intensely.

Nasaki rose from the pilot's seat and grabbed Lonny Cox. He moved the corpse, unceremoniously
shoving him in front of the instrument panel. Sitting

in the dead man's lap, Nasaki aimed the Stearman at the Hamel Nuclear Power Plant. Eight hundred feet high, Nasaki pushed the throttle into the panel and shoved the joystick forward. The plane headed toward the target.

The Stearman plunged downward like a winged meteor. Nasaki moved to the door and jumped. The craft continued its descent as the Japanese spread his arms and legs in a sky diver's position. An experienced paratrooper, who left the plane in order to see the destructive blow, he allowed himself to free-fall two hundred feet before he pulled the rip cord. A great white cloth spilled from the backpack. The chute unfolded into an enormous umbrella. Nasaki gripped the guidelines and watched the plane plunge toward the installation below.

Hirito drove the stolen Volkswagen across the field under his fellow terrorist. He smiled when he heard the roar of the Stearman's engine and saw the plane fall into the horizon. He parked the car as Nasaki's booted feet touched ground. Limping from the VW to help his partner gather up the parachute, Hirito hoped he'd hear the aircraft crash. In fact, he prayed he'd see a billowing cloud of flame-laced smoke in the distance. What a wonderful final sight before embracing death. . . .

At the Hamel plant a terrified security guard watched from his shack as the plane dropped toward the installation. He hit the general alarm button—

there was nothing else he could do. Sirens wailed. Technicians and uniformed security men raced outside only to stare dumbfounded at the descending Stearman. There was nothing they could do but stand helplessly, listening to the amplified bumble-bee hum of the craft's engine as it signaled the approach of their own destruction.

The plane smashed nose first into the front gate. A pressure plate bonded to the Stearman activated the detonator attached to a length of cord hooked up to three pounds of C-4. The bomb exploded, blowing the aircraft into chunks of metal and glass. Mangled sections of wire fencing flew into the air and the guard shack burst apart, throwing the mutilated body of the patrolman almost fifty feet. Alarm bells joined the mournful cry of the sirens as flaming debris was scattered across the compound area. . . .

A column of squad cars formed a barricade around the Hamel plant. The flashing blue lights resembled giant fireflies at night. Phoenix Force examined the wreckage. Gary Manning whistled softly, looking at the twisted wire and steel that was once a fence.

"They haven't found enough of the plane to identify it," Wade Sommer remarked. "It seems to be an old Stearman that belonged to a crop duster named Lonny Cox—of course there's so little left of the pilot we'll probably *never* have a positive ID on him.

The police checked his place. Both Cox and the plane are missing.''

"This thing wasn't just carrying insecticides," Gary declared. "It must have been full of TNT instead of DDT to cause this kind of damage."

"Thank God the plane didn't crash directly into the plant," Yakov said.

"Are they certain there isn't any damage to the reactor?" Rafael asked.

"We wouldn't be standing here if there was any doubt," Harrison Reed assured them. "Do you think this is the work of those terrorists again?"

"It's a great bloody coincidence if it isn't," David McCarter snorted, considering the NRC man's question absurd.

"Well, these Tigers of Justice or whatever they are might be Japanese fanatics," Reed said haughtily, "but I doubt one of them was willing to play kamikaze pilot and fly that thing into the plant."

"Look, Reed," the Englishman snapped. "I'm a pilot myself. I know a little about these old heaps. A fella could zoom in at one thousand feet or less— maybe six hundred if he had the nerve—and push the throttle and joystick into the panel before bailing out. Then he could parachute to safety before the plane hit its target. The bastard probably didn't consider the fact that the trajectory of the Stearman would be altered by the sudden change in weight when he jumped. That's why it missed the plant.''

"Not by much,'' Gary mused. "If it hit the center of the compound instead of the perimeter of the fence, the control center, if not the reactor dome itself, would have gone up in smoke, and there'd be a meltdown and no way to stop it.''

"The Hamel plant is a breeder,'' Reed said. "If it had an accident, all hell would break loose. Isn't that right, Professor Cohen?''

The little NRDA scientist sighed. "A breeder is the most potentially dangerous reactor because it breeds or produces more fissionable fuel. This is done by packing raw uranium around the nuclear core. This 'blanket' collects excess neutrons that leak out of the refined uranium in the center during the atom-splitting process. Thus it converts raw uranium into plutonium. This is not only the most devastating explosive—used in nuclear bombs and missiles—it also contains the most deadly forms of radiation poisoning with the greatest degree of longevity. Iodine 131, for example, attacks the thyroid glands, and strontium 90 affects bone cells. Then there is the danger of an explosion.''

"I thought a nuclear plant couldn't literally blow up,'' Yak commented.

"There is a phenomenon called a meltdown-crashdown, which can theoretically occur,'' Cohen replied. "If the lower portion of uranium melts and settles at the bottom of a reactor vessel and the upper part crashes down on it, a low-level explosion can happen. In the case of a light-water or heavy-water reactor this isn't as serious as a China Syndrome. But since the core of the breeder is surrounded by plutonium, one can't predict the results. There could be an explosion with the equivalent force of two to five hydrogen bombs.''

"Jesus," Gary said, "why do you people keep building these goddamn things?"

"Nuclear energy is no different than any other, Mr. Cartwright," Reed declared, using the Canadian's cover name. "There have been fewer accidents involving nuclear power plants than we've experienced with coal mines, oil rigs or hydroelectrical installations."

"If a coal furnace blows up, it doesn't take half the United States with it," Gary growled, his usual cool temper vanishing. "Sooner or later one of these places is going to have a major accident. Then what will you say? 'Well, a couple million people died and the air and water have been polluted for the next one hundred years, but gee, it only happened once'?"

Reed looked away nervously.

"Our main concern is the terrorists," K.O. said softly. He had remained silent until then, gazing at the police cars as though seeking information from their lights.

"How can we stop them?" Sommer asked.

"They've been one step ahead of us from the start!"

"We must determine what their next step will be," the Japanese replied simply. "And hope we guess right."

8

The telephone rang twice before Osato Goro stepped into the glass booth to answer it.

"Hello, Mr. Redding."

"Hello, Mr. Green," Donald Grover replied. "I'm glad you arrived safely. How's the weather in Salina?"

"Not as good as I'd hoped," Osato admitted.

"I warned you things in Kansas might not be as you planned."

"So you did."

"Have you heard from your friends yet?" Grover referred to the Tigers of Justice who'd been sent to infiltrate the Wadsworth plant in Iowa.

"Yes," Osato lied. "They canceled their trip for personal reasons, but they got home okay." In reality he had heard nothing from the five men and assumed they'd been killed or captured. If he confessed this to the sleeper agent, Grover might cancel their mission. Osato had planned for years to launch his vendetta against the United States, but he needed the KGB's assistance for success.

"I'm glad to hear that," Grover said. "However, the bad weather may interfere with future business activities. Will you be returning home ahead of schedule?"

"No," the Japanese answered. "I'll just have to change my plans."

"How tiresome," Grover said dryly. "Are you certain you can handle everything?"

"Yes," Osato assured him. "The weather isn't that bad. I can still complete part of my business here, and thanks to your advice, my associates have already received the material they need for the demonstration. My clients will be impressed, I'm sure."

"Let's hope so." The KGB man sighed. "I can't keep giving you advice indefinitely. I'm a busy man, you know."

"I appreciate that," the Oriental replied. "Everything promises to go well this time."

"That's happened before," Grover commented flatly. "Let's hope appearances are not deceiving this time."

"I'm certain we'll be successful, Mr. Redding."

Osato didn't wait for a reply. He hung up. The Japanese had not told Grover he sent ten Tigers of Justice to the new target. He also didn't mention that his men had purchased seven automatic rifles from a crooked arms dealer and that the Tigers planned to hijack a helicopter from a small airfield.

These actions meant the authorities would probably be unable to keep repressing the fact that the nuclear "accidents" were really deliberate sabotage. The KGB wouldn't be happy about this, since the plot had been to convince the Americans to terminate their own atomic program because of equipment failure, thereby sparing the Soviet Union possible retributions. The Russians might order SMERSH, their assassination branch, to deal with Osato Goro after the mission was over. This didn't frighten the Japanese fanatic; his hatred for the United States was greater than his desire for life.

Since childhood he had dreamed of striking back at the Yankees, who killed his father, maimed his mother and condemned him to live as a six-fingered freak. He'd been urged to have minor surgery to remove the extra digits. Osato refused. His mutation—which had never been a true physical handicap—was a constant reminder of his hatred for America. He wanted to keep his hatred alive. It was his major motivation in life.

He had laboriously planned revenge, learning English fluently, studying American customs, history, geography, politics and social structure. For years he had found others who also despised the United States and wanted to make the barbarians suffer. Thus he created the Tigers of Justice.

The radicals didn't consider themselves terrorists. They were avenging people, seeking to right the wrongs committed at Hiroshima and Nagasaki. The Tigers of Justice felt they were similar to the Israeli *Mossad* agents, who tracked down Nazis involved in the atrocities of the concentration camps. Why should American war crimes not be dealt with, as well? The Israelis weren't trying to punish all Germans for what the Nazis did more than thirty years ago. But this never occurred to the Tigers of Justice.

The uproar and protests over nuclear energy after the Three Mile Island incident inspired Osato Goro. He and his followers studied the constructions of various atomic installations and learned how to create a reactor meltdown. They formed *Anzen Sekai* to conceal their true organization while they secretly plotted and trained in the tactics of modern subversion and ancient *ninjutsu*.

At last the day of justice was at hand, and nothing would stand in their way.

Yakov Katzenelenbogen resembled a college professor as he stood before the other members of Phoenix Force and their government allies in a conference room at NRC headquarters in Washington, D.C. He tapped a grease pencil on the state of Indiana and drew a line across a map of the United States.

"Here was the first attack at the Quinton plant," he said, moving the pencil to Iowa. "Followed by the Wadsworth hit and then the Hamel installation in Kansas."

"The terrorists are moving from east to west," Rafael noticed.

"Correct," Yak said. "They haven't struck twice in the same state, so we can assume their next target will be Colorado, Nebraska or possibly Utah."

"That's a lot of territory," Wade Sommer remarked, drumming his fingers on the top of the long walnut conference table. "How can we know which nuclear installation will be the next target?"

"We can't," Gary Manning said, sipping black coffee from a plastic cup. "But we can try to guess the most likely areas and prepare for an assault by the ninjas or the Tigers of Justice or whatever you choose to call them."

"Bloody bastards," David McCarter suggested as he opened a can of cola.

"That's as good a name as any," Rafael noted with a smile.

David saluted him with the can.

Harrison Reed's expression soured. He didn't like any of the Phoenix Force—especially the Englishman and Mr. Cartwright. He'd be glad when he'd no longer have to associate with them.

Professor Cohen, however, enjoyed their company. The scientist seldom left his laboratory at the NRDA, and he had never been part of an actual manhunt before. Besides, every member of Phoenix Force had an IQ of 135 or better and could converse intelligently about a wide range of subjects. Both

Yak and Gary were excellent chess players, and K.O. was delighted to discover Cohen was familiar with go, a Japanese board game. Yes, Cohen would be sorry to have the adventure end.

For Wade Sommer, the whole business was a nightmare. Sommer hoped he would wake and discover the five antiterrorists and the Tigers of Justice were merely characters in a bad dream.

"Nebraska and Colorado seem the most likely targets," Rafael mused. He turned to Reed. "How many nuclear plants are in those two states?"

The NRC man consulted a list. "Four," he answered. Reed decided he could tolerate Rafael more than the other mavericks.

"We'll have to split up," Yak declared. "Mr. Tanaka is probably the best qualified man, since he has a better idea of what to expect from our ninja-style opponents."

"Right," Gary agreed. "If you bureaucrats can manage to put him in charge of security personnel at one of the plants, I'd say it would have top-notch protection."

K.O. stared at the Canadian, a shocked expression on his generally placid face. "I don't think...."

"You can handle a command position, my friend," Rafael assured him with a flash of flawless white teeth. "Don't belittle yourself."

The Japanese looked down at the table, embarrassed by the flattery.

"Mr. Cartwright is probably the next best choice for a commander, since he's our most experienced security man."

"Right," Gary confirmed. He wasn't boasting, merely stating a fact.

"I'd say I'm number three," Rafael said.

"Maybe I'd better go along," Sommer suggested, immediately regretting his words.

"Okay, gringo," the Cuban replied. "Just don't try to read any rules and regulations to me if I don't do everything by the book."

Sommer stifled a groan and wished he had kept his mouth shut.

"I guess that leaves you and me, Mr. Goldberg," David said. "Think we can manage, old boy?"

"I hope so, Mr. Masters," Yak said, smiling thinly.

David McCarter glanced up at the Janson Nuclear Power Plant and sighed. All atomic installations seemed identical. He was tired of looking at great chimney shapes and overgrown ostrich eggs. Yet reactors varied, and how they operated depended on the plant's function. Security precautions were different, too. The Janson installation had not neglected this matter. There were alarms, heat sensors, television monitors and electrical eyes everywhere. The guards were competent and better trained than most rent-a-cops. All had military or police background and qualified on the range with their service revolvers four times a year.

If the Englishman had been in charge of the Tigers of Justice, he wouldn't have picked the Janson plant for a target. Yet the terrorists had managed to infiltrate "foolproof" security before. David checked the guard positions to be certain none of the men was napping. Dressed in a British commando jacket, fatigue trousers and boots, with an Ingram M-10 machine pistol strapped to his shoulder and the Browning in a hip holster, he presented a formidable professional appearance. That's what he intended when he selected the outfit.

David was pleased to discover all the security personnel were alert and ready for action, willing to follow orders given by the Briton or Yakov. But the clouded Colorado sky seemed to favor the black-clad ninja saboteurs. David couldn't shake a sense of nervous apprehension.

He and Yak had stationed themselves at the installation three days before, but nothing had happened. They contacted their fellow Phoenix Force members, and the other plants were also incident-free. Maybe the terrorists had given up. David scoffed at his own thoughts. *You always assume a fanatic won't quit until the bastard is dead.*

The harsh sound of giant blades slicing air caught the Englishman's attention. He turned to gaze at the twin sunlamps that burned through the black sky as they approached. Shoe leather slapped concrete and the guards scrambled to their positions, some drawing side arms. Two men carried pump shotguns. The outline of the helicopter materialized above the plant. David located Yak and hurried to join the Israeli.

"That isn't a police chopper," he told his partner.

"We can't assume it's the terrorists, either," Yak replied. "If we jump to conclusions, we might kill an innocent, overcurious, civilian pilot."

Dressed in a gray turtleneck and baggy chinos, the senior member of Phoenix Force carried a small LAW rocket launcher. Made of light plastic and fiberglass, the LAW fires a formidable minimissile that can pierce a tank and blast its crew into bloodied jelly. They selected the rocket launcher in case the Tigers attempted another aerial assault, since the only way to deal with such an attack would be to blow the descending aircraft to bits before it crashed into the plant.

"Unless the pilot is totally daft and has one hell of a death wish, he won't dive into us," McCarter said. "There's no way he could parachute to safety. That copter can't be more than three hundred feet above ground."

"He might plan to hover over the reactor and drop grenades on it," the Israeli mused. "They might even have a grenade launcher on board."

"Christ," David muttered. "An HE shell could

blow open that son of a bitch like a balloon full of water!''

Yak grunted agreement as he raised the LAW to his left shoulder, using the prosthetic arm to brace the barrel while his flesh-and-bone fingers moved to the push-button trigger mechanism. He watched the chopper through elevated sights.

The Janson plant used a light-water reactor. That meant the uranium within the vessel was cooled to a stable level by circulating ordinary water into the core. If the metal skin of the reactor dome was ruptured and the water gushed out, a nuclear meltdown would be irreversible.

They waited tensely. The gaping muzzle of the LAW tracked the chopper as it slowly swung over the installation. Then the helicopter rose sharply and turned away from the Janson plant.

"Must have got lost," David remarked, his hands still locked around the frame of his Ingram.

"Perhaps," Yak replied, lowering the LAW. "And maybe we've just witnessed a variation of an old ninja trick K.O. told us about."

"The kites with the dummies on them," the Englishman recalled. "It's a distraction for the real assault!"

"Check the area!" Katzenelenbogen shouted at the security personnel. "The terrorists may have entered while our attention was on the helicopter!"

The guards responded, dashing in all directions,

weapons in hand. One officer ran toward the base of a turbogenerator silo, holding his Smith & Wesson .38 high. A shadow with arms and legs appeared from the corner. Before the guard could react, the M-16 in the ninja's gloved hands spit a stream of .223-caliber death. The force of the automatic-rifle rounds sent the patrolman hurtling backward, blood dripping from his bullet-riddled chest.

The Tigers of Justice were inside the plant.

9

The terrorist with the M-16 didn't live long enough to gloat about his kill. Another Janson security guard saw his compatriot fall and rushed to the turbo-generator. The ninja turned toward the new opponent as the patrolman's riot gun boomed. A blast of 12-gauge buckshot smashed into the black-cloaked assassin, throwing his shattered corpse against the wall of the silo.

Something whistled from the shadows, and a metal disk slammed into the security guard's face. The sharp points of the star-shaped weapon pierced the man's cheek, and one stabbed deep into his left eyeball. With a scream the patrolman dropped his shotgun and staggered back, clawing at the *shaken* lodged in his face.

David McCarter reached the silo and fired a quick burst of Ingram lead into the darkness. A howl rewarded his efforts. The second ninja stumbled into view, and the Englishman triggered another volley of 9mm rounds into the terrorist. The Tiger of Justice collapsed in a twitching heap.

The metallic rattle of automatic rifles mingled with the deep-throated roars of shotguns and service revolvers. A ninja invader cut down two Janson security men before a guard pumped two .357 slugs into him. Another terrorist, armed with an autopistol, fired three .380 bullets into a burly patrolman. The guard seemed to absorb the projectiles as he walked closer and raised his .38 Colt Diamondback. He shot the ninja in the face. Both men fell.

Two Tigers of Justice crept to the office building. Despite the unexpected reception by the plant's defenders, the fanatics still hoped to enter the control room and blow it apart with RDX mines. One set a magnetic charge against the steel door as the other stood guard with an M-16 in his hands.

"Don't you boys believe in knocking?" Yakov asked, stepping out from the corner of the building.

The Colt Commander in his left hand barked. A heavy 200-grain .45-caliber bullet slammed into the center of the closest terrorist's chest. The man's arms shot up, hurling the M-16 as though eager to discard the weapon. His lifeless body crashed to the ground as his partner jerked a Charter Arms .38 revolver from a shoulder holster. Yak's Colt boomed again and the ninja's head exploded like a blood-filled melon.

David McCarter jogged around the base of the second turbogenerator, his M-10 held ready. Suddenly he saw two figures struggling in the dimness by the silo. Rushing forward, the Englishman discovered a black-garbed killer had wrapped a wire garrote around a Janson security patrolman's neck. The ninja was strangling his victim.

The Briton couldn't fire at the terrorist without endangering the guard. Besides, he wanted to take the invader alive if possible. He moved rapidly and tried to slam the frame of the Ingram into the black-hooded head. The ninja swiftly released the guard and weaved out of the path of David's attack.

The security man wilted to the ground as the terrorist nimbly caught the lapel of McCarter's jacket with one hand and a sleeve with the other. Using the Briton's own momentum, the ninja dropped to the ground and pulled David forward. The killer's back touched the ground, and he raised a foot to McCarter's midsection. The saboteur executed a *tomoenage*, a circle throw. He straightened his knee and sent his opponent hurtling head over heels.

David hit the pavement hard, slapping an arm to the concrete to break his fall. The sudden impact jarred his spine, and the Ingram slipped from his numb fingers. He looked up to see the ninja already on his feet. The blade of a dagger flashed in a gloved fist as the terrorist prepared to finish off the Briton.

The ninja bent to complete his lunge. David braced his back and swung a leg high. His boot connected with the killer's face, kicking his mouth hard. The blow propelled the terrorist backward. He staggered and fell to one knee. Dazed, the ninja managed to retain his knife. He cocked back his arm to throw it.

McCarter's hand streaked to his hip. Flicking open the holster's retaining strap, he quickly drew the Browning automatic and rolled on his belly. The Englishman snap aimed and squeezed the trigger twice. Two 9mm hollowpoint slugs drilled into the ninja's chest like murderous metal hornets. The knife fell from limp fingers, and the terrorist slumped to the ground and died.

A black-clad invader discovered the LAW Yak discarded during the fight. Aware he'd perish in the process, the terrorist took the rocket launcher, placed it on his shoulder and prepared to fire on the reactor dome.

A shot snarled from the office building and a fat .45 bullet hit the ninja in the pit of his stomach. The force of the slug knocked the man to the pavement. Yak ran closer, the Commander in hand.

Driven by a true fanatic's determination, the terrorist dragged himself to one knee and picked up the LAW. He aimed the muzzle at the reactor. The Israeli had no choice. He fired two more .45 rounds into the ninja.

"Yak?" David called as he jogged over to his partner.

"Yes, *Mr. Masters*," the Israeli replied, reminding McCarter about their cover names.

David shrugged. "The guards are still checking to see if any of these creepy crawlers are still around, but I think you got the last one."

"Did we take any of them alive?"

The Englishman rolled his eyes. "We're bloody lucky to be alive. The bastards fought like lunatics. How the hell did they get through the security systems?"

"Ninja magic," Yak said grimly, holstering his pistol. "We'd better find its secret—and soon."

The other members of Phoenix Force and Wade Sommer joined David and Yak at the Janson installation the next morning. Rafael Encizo entered the room and smiled at his companions.

"I don't know how those ninjas got into the other plants," he said, "but I can tell you how they managed to break in here last night."

The Cuban enjoyed a dramatic pause, watching their expressions as they waited for the answer.

"Through the sewer system."

"What?" Wade Sommer said, glaring at him.

"They popped out of a manhole at the back of the turbogenerators like a bunch of gophers," Rafael replied, sinking into a leather armchair. "They must have had a tough time squeezing through the narrow drain pipe, but that's how they did it."

"Ninja magic," David snorted as he dropped an empty cola can into a wastebasket.

"Lousy security," Gary Manning added. The Canadian sat behind the desk jotting notes on a pad.

"Since the danger of radioactive contamination is so great, even the plumbing system is supposed to be sealed off from public sewers," Keio Ohara explained, resting a leg on the corner of the desk. "Used water is cycled through filters and solutions of alcohol and salt before it is released. Apparently this installation failed to include this precaution when it was built."

"The Wadsworth plant had a major security flaw, too," Yak added. "Although the front entrance was guarded and the main door to the control room was operated by a voiceprint computer, the fire exit didn't even have a burglar alarm. The terrorists burned through with a blow torch. But how did they know about it?"

"These Tigers of Justice seem to have ESP," Rafael remarked. "Remember one of the surveillance cameras was out of order when we visited the Wadsworth plant? I bet you a bushel of chili peppers the terrorists climbed the section of fence monitored by that camera."

"I've been thinking about that, Mr. Sanchez," Gary replied. "In fact, I contacted the maintenance department at Wadsworth and asked what caused the camera to malfunction. They told me a fuse blew and somehow burned out some circuits. They'd never seen anything like it."

"Another curious 'accident,' eh?" David commented as he began to pace the room.

"Is it possible the camera was rigged to go haywire?" Sommer asked.

"No problem there," Gary answered. "If someone inserted a magnesium rod into it with a small detonator, it could even be set to go off forty-eight hours later."

"You suspect someone sabotaged the camera in advance?" Sommer asked.

"I'm suggesting the terrorists not only know the weak points of each installation, they also take advantage of convenient 'malfunctions' of security devices," the Canadian answered.

"Somebody working in the plants has been helping the bastards," David agreed.

"Someone who was in the plants," Gary corrected. "Unless that person is an even bigger fanatic than the Tigers of Justice, he wouldn't stick around when a reactor meltdown was due to occur."

"But how could the terrorists get accomplices in so many different plants all over the country?" Sommer asked.

"Perhaps they didn't need to," Rafael remarked. "A security or safety inspector for the Nuclear Regulatory Commission would be going from state to state checking various installations, no?"

"The federal government doesn't issue top-security clearances casually," the Justice Department man declared. "I can't believe anyone responsible enough to pass the background checks would willingly assist a bunch of crazies in black Halloween costumes!"

"Governments make mistakes," Yakov stated. "I think we better contact Mr. Reed and get a list of every NRC official who's recently been to any of the plants attacked by the saboteurs."

"And the names of visitors—official or otherwise—from each installation," Gary added. "It would take a sly fox, but somebody masquerading as a journalist might be able to disable security equipment and gather information to feed to the terrorists."

"Well, we don't have any other leads." Sommer sighed. "The FBI didn't find a goddamn thing about the dead Tigers of Justice. Immigration and Customs people haven't found any evidence that those clowns entered the country illegally. Interpol now has their fingerprints and dental X rays and they're looking into it. But by the time they come up with anything, the Tigers of Justice will probably be old enough to collect social security."

"Only if they become American citizens," Rafael commented with a smile, "and the federal government doesn't use it up first."

"Let's worry about the Tigers of Justice for now," Gary said. "We've got our work cut out for us. While we check out possible terrorist allies, we still have to try to guess their next move."

"That won't be easy this time," the Israeli said. "After last night they'll probably change their strategy. The Tigers won't follow such an obvious pattern. They might strike at any nuclear plant in the United States."

"Most curious," K.O. muttered. He'd noticed the morning newspaper on the manager's desk and discovered something of interest on the front page.

"If it concerns a controversial political subject, don't mention it," the Cuban urged.

"Osato Goro and his *Anzen Sekai* group held a rally near the Hamel plant yesterday," the Oriental explained.

"Isn't he the Japanese chap who was leading the demonstration at the Quinton plant when we were there?" David asked.

K.O. nodded. "It is an odd coincidence that Osato-san and his organization came to this country at the same time as the Tigers of Justice."

"Maybe *too* odd a coincidence," Rafael said grimly. "This Osato character had a rally at the Quinton plant and now he's at the Hamel installation."

"Let's not jump to conclusions," Gary urged. "After all, it's common for antinuke folks to assemble near a site that's recently had an accident."

"Makes you wonder how scared they really are," David muttered sourly.

"Or how strong their feelings are that they're willing to expose themselves to what they fear,'' Yak commented.

"In the case of Osato Goro,'' K.O. began, ''the question is not how passionately he opposes nuclear energy but to what extremes he and his group are willing to go to.''

"Yeah,'' Gary said flatly. "And whether *Anzen Sekai* has another, less public title—the Tigers of Justice.''

10

Rafael Encizo sighed with relief as the 747 touched down on the runway. He turned to Keio Ohara, who was still sitting beside him in the first-class section of the airplane.

"I'll be glad to get my luggage off this thing," Rafael confessed. "Without my sharp little friend resting at the small of my back I feel helpless."

K.O. agreed. He understood his partner's attachment to his knife. Although he was trained to use many weapons, only one held great meaning for him. It was a *katana* given to K.O. by his *sensi*—martial arts instructor—in recognition of his achievements in kendo, a sport form of Japanese fencing. The long, two-hand sword of the samurai warrior was almost three hundred years old. Yet its flawless steel blade was incredibly sharp. Unlike Rafael, K.O. did not carry his beloved weapon into action. The sword served little practical purpose. Besides, K.O. feared it might be lost or damaged in combat.

"It is fortunate we have special-agent credentials from the Justice Department," he stated. "Or we might have had difficulty getting our firearms on the plane.''

"I hope Sommer's hombres have that van ready for us, and I hope they managed to stock it with the equipment we requested.''

"We may not need it," the Japanese said. "But if we do and we don't have it, to improvise would be most difficult.''

Rafael frowned. "Have you wondered why Osato and his group decided to have a rally in Arizona? That's a long way from Kansas. Could be the Tigers of Justice plan to launch their next assault in a southwestern state.''

"It is possible," K.O. agreed, "if there is a connection between the terrorists and *Anzen Sekai.*''

The Cuban smiled broadly. "You know, it will be ironic if our mission comes to an end in this city.''

His companion grinned in return. Their plane had just landed in Phoenix, Arizona.

Sakata Fujo looked at Osato Goro with admiration as his commander lectured passionately to antinuke demonstrators in the auditorium of Colibri University. Although Sakata understood little English, he recognized the emotional quality of Osato's voice and gestures, and he noticed the effect his speech had on the audience. Indeed, Osato-san was a master of the art of persuasion. His verbal and strategic skills made him a brilliant leader—just as Sakata Fujo was an excellent choice for second-in-command.

Sakata felt an even greater hatred for Americans and their atomic toys than Osato. The Sakatas were a poor family who lived along the Sea of Japan in the city of Nagasaki. His mother's back and legs had been scarred for life by radiation burns, and his father died of cancer, possibly the result of exposure to the bomb. Fujo was born blind in one eye, his sister entered the world with no arms and legs and three other siblings had been stillborn, their tiny bodies twisted monstrosities—mutilated by the nuclear poison in their parents' genes.

Sakata Nitobe, Fujo's uncle and a successful karate instructor in Kyoto, took the boy at age fourteen. Realizing the heartache and bitterness in Fujo's heart, Sakata Nitobe hoped to give him confidence, discipline, understanding and fulfillment through martial arts. Fujo proved an apt student, studying and practicing with a zeal that pleased his uncle— until he learned why his nephew wished to excel in unarmed combat: Fujo wanted to kill Americans.

Sakata Nitobe refused to continue teaching Fujo when he discovered this. Recognizing the principles and morality of martial artists, Fujo enrolled into another *dojo* and concealed his true goals from his new *sensei*, "master." The bitter youth became a cunning man with a deadly weapon in each limb and the reflexes of a panther to wield them.

When Osato Goro formed the Tigers of Justice, he

put Sakata in charge of the group's self-defense program. A self-taught authority of *ninjutsu*, Fujo later instructed the cult in the deadly arts of the sinister espionage agents of feudal Japan.

Like Osato, he had no qualms about working with the KGB. If the Russians were enemies of the United States, Sakata welcomed their assistance. He felt the Soviet Union developed their own nuclear weapons and plants only to protect themselves from the Yankee imperialists. In fact, Sakata hoped the KGB would recruit him as a SMERSH assassin—and assign him to kill Americans.

"In 1957, the International Atomic Energy Commission was formed to prevent the spread of nuclear weapons," Osato Goro said. The crowd was ten times larger than the first rally at the Quinton plant. Reports of reactor malfunctions and near tragic "accidents" attracted more people to the antinuke side. "It has the authority to inspect any atomic installation in the world if the plant's products are intended for military use. Yet even the nations who signed the Nuclear Nonproliferation Treaty are not compelled to submit to such inspections, and the IAEC has no authority to do anything if they find irregularities. This is the world's safeguard against a nuclear holocaust!"

Osato put his six-fingered hands on the lectern and glared at his audience. "Of course, the IAEC has no authority to inspect industrial or privately owned nuclear power plants. Not that it matters. The Nuclear Nonproliferation Treaty is a worthless scrap of paper. It has not stopped Canada, France, England, the Soviet Union, West Germany or the United States from selling atomic materials.

"Your country has sold uranium and, in some cases, plutonium to such repressive dictatorships as South Korea, Taiwan, the Philippines, Argentina, Brazil, South Africa and Spain, when it was still under the fascist rule of Francisco Franco. It helped construct nuclear reactors in Israel and Egypt *before* they signed their peace agreement! During American involvement in Vietnam, your government even built a small atomic reactor in Da Lat. Unless the import and export of radioactive goods is brought to a halt, nuclear war is an unquestionable certainty!"

The audience shifted uneasily in its chairs and gasped fearfully at such a grim fate. The Japanese resisted a smile. He couldn't see faces through the flare of the stage lights, but he knew what expressions they wore.

"Recently we have seen that the unstable elements of radioactive death need not be in bombs or missiles to threaten mankind," he continued. "The malfunctions and accidents at nuclear power plants have occurred with alarming frequency, indicating construction and safety precautions in these installations will not withstand the test of time. This fact is disturbing enough, but with the increase of international terrorism we see an even more frightened threat lurking in the future.

"How many of you are aware that literally thousands of tons of deadly radioactive materials have 'disappeared' from plants or during transportation by truck or train? A ship carrying almost two hundred tons of uranium oxide vanished in the 1960s. The captain and crew were never seen again. It is believed this uranium wound up in Israel and was used in the construction of that country's first nuclear bomb. What about the rest that remains unaccounted for? Are a band of fanatics building their own atomic weapons this very second?

"Ah, this would require the assistance of a nuclear physicist, you might say. Yet a young chemistry student made a design for a functional atomic bomb using unclassified literature as his reference. Acquiring the substances for such a weapon is not difficult. Even natural uranium can be refined by gas centrifuge methods. If terrorists could seize plutonium, they'd have a fearful weapon that need not explode to be deadly. Ground into powder, it could be released from a plane into the atmosphere over any major city. There is an estimated seven million pounds of plutonium in the world. A single pound contains enough radiation poisoning to kill every man, woman and child in the entire world.

"And what of the nuclear power plants themselves? There have already been numerous attempts to sabotage such installations. Arson nearly caused a nuclear tragedy at a plant in New York State. A bomb was discovered and deactivated at a plant in Wisconsin. Another was found near a 'research' reactor at the University of Illinois. Sabotage devices did explode at two nuclear power plants in France in 1975, although neither resulted in a reactor melt-down. The Israeli air forces bombed the construction site of a nuclear reactor in Iraq. Who can say a group of fanatics won't one day use a similar tactic in the United States?

"The threat of nuclear power—in any form—is too dangerous to accept for any reason. There are numerous energy alternatives available. Solar power can be utilized by improving the technology of storage cells and batteries. The lowly windmill can be used to power electrical generators. Geothermal and ocean thermal heat generated by molten rock layers and tropical waters have great potential as a source of energy. Tidal waves can also be used to power engines. Even garbage can be reprocessed to serve as fuel—something my country has been doing for years. Although coal and oil present problems for the environment, they do not contain radioactive mate-rial that can cause an atomic disaster or provide radicals with fearsome weapons.

"The nuclear establishment cannot be permitted to continue making profits while endangering the entire world. It is time to tell the merchants of destruction we will not stand for this madness. Join in this cause, or tell your children you do not care if they are doomed to inherit a nuclear nightmare instead of a sane safe world." Osato bowed deeply. "I thank you."

The audience, rising from its chairs, responded with enthusiastic applause. The Japanese bowed again before he walked offstage. To his surprise he saw a neatly dressed Oriental waiting in the wings. Even taller than Sakata Fujo, the stranger stood beside the second-in-command of *Anzen Sekai*, his expression patient.

"Osato-san," Sakata explained. "This is Tanaka Demura from the *Tokyo News*. He wishes to speak with you about our mission in the United States."

"*Konnichiwa*, Tanaka-san," Osato said, bowing graciously. "Good afternoon, Mr. Tanaka. It is a pleasure to meet you."

"*Arigato*," Keio Ohara replied as he returned the gesture. "Thank you. The honor is truly mine, Osato-san. May I compliment you on your mastery of English. To express yourself so well in a foreign tongue is indeed worthy testimony to your linguistic abilities."

"You speak English, Tanaka-san?"

"*Hai*. Yes. That is why my editors sent me here, although I lack your command of the language."

"I am glad you appreciate my proficiency in English." Osato smiled thinly. "What do you think of the meaning of my words?"

"As a newspaper reporter it is not my task to express my opinion," K.O. answered. "I seek only to accurately record facts and deliver them to my editors."

"Forgive me," Osato sighed, "but I've found few journalists report anything impartially."

"I do my best, Osato-san."

"Very well," the other man said. "If you understand what I told my listeners, you should understand the goal of *Anzen Sekai*. We oppose the use of nuclear energy in any form and advocate a total ban on atomic weapons and demand all nuclear power plants—military or civilian—be shut down and dismantled."

"What would be done with the radioactive materials taken from the reactors?" K.O. inquired. "Dealing with atomic waste is a major problem for nuclear installations. Burying it or dropping it into the ocean—even sealed in special containers—clearly presents hazards to the environment. Most plants try to recycle nuclear wastes for this very reason."

"A very astute question, Tanaka-san," Osato said. "I propose the materials be segregated into high-level and low-level radiation and sealed in special vats of similar construction as a reactor vessel. Remote areas should be selected for the 'grave sites' of these deadly products. Deserts, tundras or uninhabited islands would be ideal."

K.O. smiled. "Wouldn't these sites be tempting

targets for 'grave robbers' wishing to acquire nuclear weapons?''

"Of course," Osato agreed. "The sites would have to be heavily guarded. No government could be trusted to police its own atomic products, so special troops would be assigned by the United Nations."

"If one trusts the United Nations," K.O. said dryly. "I assume you also feel all the world's governments will submit to this program and none will conceal uranium and plutonium for future use?"

"This will probably happen," Osato admitted. "Thus international organizations like the IAEC would have to be given authority to inspect and regulate such misconduct throughout the world."

"I see."

"You do not approve?"

"It is not my place to form an opinion."

"But you have one nonetheless. Tell me."

"Your proposal seems impractical, Osato-san," K.O. answered. "Forgive my bluntness, but your plan would require either a utopian world or an international police state. Unfortunately the first shall never exist, and hopefully neither will the other."

"So you favor nuclear power," Sakata muttered.

"Perhaps the world would be a better place if the atom had never been split and harnessed for energy," K.O. replied. "But the reality of nuclear power cannot be wiped away by wishes. It is naive to believe the nations of the world will discard their nuclear weapons. Thus the production of such devices is, and shall remain, necessary for each country's national defense. Still, safety is a critical issue—and one that cannot be overlooked. Perhaps, as our technology improves, nuclear fission plants can be converted to a fusion system. Instead of splitting atoms, the fusion process links atomic nuclei together and creates heavier, more stable atoms. A fusion reactor would be safer and easier to manage. This might provide nuclear power with a minimum of risk.''

"Your knowledge of this subject impresses me, Tanaka-san," Osato said stiffly. "However, fusion reactors are still in the experimental stages. The threat of nuclear destruction exists now, and we cannot wait until the year 2000 to deal with it. If the nations of the world tried to cooperate, the 'impossible utopia' you scoff at could be a reality. The best way to start is by an international effort to end the proliferation of atomic plants and weapons, with the goal of a total nuclear ban in the future.''

"I meant no disrespect, Osato-san," K.O. assured him. "But you did ask my opinion.''

"Indeed, I insisted," the leader of *Anzen Sekai* admitted. "My tour in this country has come at an appropriate time. Recently there have been some terrible accidents at several American nuclear plants. The atomic energy conglomerates have managed to suppress information about these incidents, but it is believed several lives have been lost and at least one reactor meltdown nearly occurred. A plane crash at an installation in Kansas is evidence the improbable is not impossible. Thousands of concerned Americans are heeding my warning. The prospect of an organized effort to outlaw nuclear energy appears most promising.''

''I'll relay this to my readers in your exact words,'' Keio Ohara promised. ''One more question, please. Do you think it is conceivable that one or more of these accidents may actually be the work of terrorists? Perhaps the PLO or a group similar to the SDS, the Hanafi Muslims or the Tigers of Justice are responsible.''

Osato Goro's expression remained calm, concealing the shock of hearing his secret organization's name uttered by a journalist. Sakata Fujo, however, was unable to hide his surprise. His eyes widened and his mouth dropped.

''It is possible,'' Osato answered. ''The nuclear establishment seems determined to suppress the truth about these incidents, and that may be the reason. If so, it is stronger motivation for doing away with such installations.''

''I see,'' K.O. nodded. *''Arigato.''* He bowed deeply, but his eyes never left the two men. ''Thank you. You have been most generous with your time. I shall not detain you any longer.''

''May your return to Tokyo be a safe one, Tanaka-san.'' Osato returned the bow.

The tall Japanese turned and walked to the exit at the end of the corridor. Sakata turned to his commander, urgency written on his face.

"I could kill him now," he whispered. "Silently. With my bare hands."

"What would that accomplish?" Osato replied.

"He knows about us!"

"He knows of the Tigers of Justice. Perhaps he learned of it from a source in Nippon or an information leak from the American government. One of our members may have been foolish enough to take his banner on a mission. They regard those decorative bits of cloth as talismans that will give them some sort of mystical abilities."

"He knows," Sakata insisted.

"That makes little difference," Osato said. "After tomorrow the whole world will know of the Tigers of Justice."

"Your plan is very dangerous, Osato-san," Sakata commented, a trace of apprehension in his voice.

"*Hai,*" the terrorist leader agreed. "But it is obvious we cannot leave the job to others. We must do it ourselves. Even if we perish in the process, we will create the most devastating nuclear incident in the history of the world and the Americans shall have their own Hiroshima—but it will be a thousand times worse."

11

The dark van looked normal. Thousands of such vehicles can be found in the United States. Because of their ability to carry large loads, these machines are a favorite among companies.

However, few vans feature a specially modified engine able to accelerate from thirty-five miles an hour to one hundred as quickly as a sports car. The surveillance equipment—police-scanner radio, periscope with infrared lens, built-in Watts-line telephone and an assortment of weaponry—also made the rig unique. Of course, most vans aren't furnished by the Justice Department to serve the need of Phoenix Force.

Rafael Encizo sat in a folding chair, filing his nails with his pet knife, while Keio Ohara looked through the periscope that extended from the roof, disguised as an air vent. The night viewer provided artificial daylight. The periscope allowed K.O. to watch the front of the Stanton Hotel in downtown Phoenix at 10:00 P.M.

"You say the man with Osato seemed pretty upset

when you mentioned the Tigers of Justice?" the Cuban asked.

"Yes," K.O. replied, his right eye fixed to the periscope. "I'm almost certain *Anzen Sekai* is connected with the terrorists."

"That doesn't mean Osato will lead us to the others tonight." Rafael sighed.

"He will try to contact them," the Japanese stated firmly. "You followed him after he left the university, and he didn't talk to anyone or use a telephone before returning to his hotel."

"But we've got his room bugged and his phone tapped and we haven't heard a thing. He may have slipped out another exit."

"True," K.O. admitted. "We cannot watch everything, and he may use a pay phone inside. What other choice do we have?"

"Well, we may as well break this surveillance business into shifts," Rafael suggested. "Since you seem eager to stay up, I think I'll take a nap...."

"There they are," K.O. stated. His tone revealed none of the excitement and anticipation he felt as Osato Goro and Sakata Fujo emerged from the building.

"Is he headed for the Ford?" Rafael asked anxiously.

"He and Fujo just got into it."

"*Bueno.*" The Cuban smiled. "Give me the keys to the van."

"There is no need to use the periscope now," the Japanese said. "I can drive."

"I know how you drive," Rafael replied. "We want to tail those two without being seen. You get a little reckless behind the wheel, my friend."

"I'll be careful," K.O. vowed, reluctant to surrender the keys.

"If the cops are chasing us for speeding, we'll attract more attention than a nun in a whorehouse," Rafael insisted. "Give me the keys."

With a sigh the Japanese obliged.

The van discreetly followed Osato's car. Rafael kept enough distance between the Phoenix Force vehicle and the Ford to avoid making the terrorists suspicious. Occasionally he allowed other cars to pull in front, but he never lost sight of Osato's little car. The Ford followed Route 17 and entered the freeway, leaving Phoenix, Arizona, behind.

When Osato drove along the desert region, Rafael decreased speed to let them gain distance. Finally the Ford turned onto a seldom used dirt path. The Cuban killed the headlights as he pursued the other vehicle.

"Look through the periscope and let me know if I'm going off the road, K.O.," Rafael told his partner. "I can still see their taillights, but not much else."

With the aid of the scope the van tracked the car

until it pulled off the road and headed toward a small farmhouse. Since they knew where Osato would be, Rafael stopped the big green machine and backed up until their vehicle was out of sight.

K.O. and Rafael emerged from the van. The Cuban carried a Belgian FLN automatic rifle. A superb weapon with a dependable 7.62mm cartridge and excellent accuracy, the FLN was a fine choice for sniper operations. His partner held a device that resembled a harpoon gun, with a telescopic sight mounted on the barrel. K.O. personally designed the high-powered air gun. Although the CO_2 cartridge in the breech propelled a projectile with impressive accuracy up to one hundred and fifty feet, the rifle was not a weapon. It launched a small wireless microphone attached to a steel arrowhead.

Both men imitated the Executioner's favorite combat uniform: black fatigues, their faces smeared with black camouflage paint. They also had Starlite binoculars. Similar to the design of the periscope, the infrared field glasses converted a pitch-black night into early dusk.

Thanks to the Starlites, the Phoenix Force members were able to examine the farmhouse from a distance. Six automobiles were parked near the building. All were small, well-treated vehicles, suggesting they were rentals like Osato's Ford. Although no guard was outside the house, K.O. and Rafael approached with extreme caution. Both were adept at moving silently in the dark, and they automatically favored the shadows for extra cover. One hundred feet from the house, Rafael stopped and adopted a prone position. He put the stock of his FLN snugly against his shoulder and pointed the weapon at the door of the dwelling.

Confident his partner would provide cover fire if needed, K.O. advanced. Seventy-five feet from the house, K.O. raised his air gun and carefully aimed. He squeezed the trigger. A mild hiss escaped from the muzzle of the rifle. The CO_2 powered projectile found its mark, the arrowhead biting firmly into the wooden sill of the window.

The Phoenix Force pair withdrew from the house, returning to the van. K.O. donned a headset, turned up the radio receiver and listened to the voices transmitted by the microphone lodged in the farmhouse.

Osato Goro stood in the center of the modestly furnished living room. Thirteen of his followers gazed up at him, their silent faces revealing eagerness to hear their master's voice. Eight of the Tigers of Justice were already stationed at their next target, preparing for their final mission. Fifteen Tigers were killed or captured during assaults on the other plants. Of the original thirty-seven members, twenty-two remained.

The leader of the terrorists pushed these thoughts from his consciousness. He knew there would be casualties when he launched his war against the American atomic establishment—and some of the losses might be his followers. Every Tiger of Justice knew the risks involved and accepted the dangers. They were willing to die for their cause—some were even eager to do so. Osato was indifferent about his survival, so he experienced little sorrow over the death of his followers. In Osato's mind they died for an honorable cause. No man can do more than live and die with his beliefs.

"My brothers," he said to the cult in their native language. "Our struggle against the American nuclear conspirators is swiftly coming to an end. You have all waited for many years for the day of vengeance upon this country for the atrocities at Hiroshima and Nagasaki. You have studied and trained for this hour of judgment—and now, at last, that time is here."

Inside the van, K.O.'s expression hardened as he listened to the speech through his headset. Osato Goro wasn't merely associated with the Tigers of Justice: he was their leader!

"Everyone in this room has suffered because of the callous actions of the American government at the end of World War II," Osato continued. "Many of you, like me, have endured disfigurement since birth because the barbarians heartlessly bombed innocent civilians. All of us have seen loved ones scarred by radiation. You've known the anguish of the atomic curse. Yet others do not. The world does not care about what happened at Hiroshima and Nagasaki. Now we shall remind them and show the Americans their nuclear program is a two-edged sword that can be wielded against its master."

"We will strike like the tiger to claim justice!" the terrorists replied in a collective voice, proudly saying the cult's motto.

"Hai," Osato smiled. "Yes. Our actions tomorrow will avenge our suffering...and it will serve another purpose. We all know how the Americans occupied Nippon after the war. They virtually ruled our country and forced their crude culture on our people. The Tigers of Justice will show the world that the true spirit of Japan still lives. We are the children of the atomic holocaust, victims of the harsh technology of the twentieth century. Yet we have not swayed from the traditional ways of our ancestors. Our courageous slain brothers will be martyrs of an honored cause, and history will one day acknowledge our efforts as the beginning of a turnabout in Japanese culture. Our people will eventually shun their role as imitation Americans and return to the principles and ideals of *bushido*."

K.O.'s dark eyes burned with anger as he listened to the speech. "Do not speak of *bushido*, you mad dog," he hissed.

"Osato-sama," said Nasaki, the harelipped Tiger of Justice, addressing his leader as Lord Osato.

"Will we not need more weapons to accomplish our goal? Of the seven automatic rifles acquired in Colorado, only three remain."

"We shall have more weapons," Osato assured him. "Our benefactor has already supplied them to our brothers who wait for us at our next target."

"It is curious that a *Beikoku-jin* would assist us in our mission," Myoshibi Haro, a short Japanese remarked suspiciously.

"He serves us to ease his guilt-ridden conscience," Osato explained. "And he has served us well, has he not?"

"Hai," Hirito, the fanatic with the clubfoot agreed. "These explosives were hidden in the fireplace just as he said."

"Do not worry about our American ally," the ringleader told his men. "He will not betray us. This will be our last mission, so we must not fail. When we—"

"What is this?" Nasaki interrupted his boss. The terrorist stared out a window at the oversized metal spearhead lodged in the sill.

Several members of the cult rushed to investigate. Haro, a transistor specialist, recognized the purpose of the aluminum bulb above the projectile's blade. "It's a short-range wireless microphone," he explained. "Someone is listening to us!"

Osato responded instantly. "The intruders can't be far away. Find them. Try to spare at least one for interrogation, but kill them if you must."

12

"We've been discovered," Keio Ohara calmly told his partner. "Perhaps we should leave."

"*Cristo!*" Rafael Encizo exclaimed, scrambling to the driver's seat. "'Perhaps we should leave,' he says. What else would we do? Tell them we're testing out a new mobile lunch wagon that serves sushi?"

The Cuban turned the key in the ignition and the engine roared to life. He shifted gears and stomped on the gas pedal. The van lunged forward. Rafael executed a hasty U-turn and sent the vehicle flying up the dirt path toward the main road.

The Tigers of Justice bolted from the farmhouse and ran to the cars. Osato ordered Sakata Fujo and five others to remain as the other terrorists climbed into their vehicles.

"We have things to do here before we leave," the leader explained. "Whatever happens, some of us must deliver the explosives to our brothers and see that our mission succeeds."

"We cannot abandon our comrades," Myoshibi Haro stated.

"We do not know how many enemy are out there," Osato replied coldly. "If they are few in number, our brothers will deal with them. If they are many, it is best we lose no more men than we must."

"You would let them serve as decoys to allow us to escape?" Haro said, his voice revealing his contempt.

"Nothing can be permitted to stand in the way of our mission," the leader declared in a flat hard voice.

Haro turned to his fellow Tigers of Justice. He knew Sakata was as fanatical as Osato, so he addressed the four men in his own peer group.

"We have often talked of devotion to our cause and loyalty to our brotherhood," he said. "Where is this loyalty if we care nothing of our own kind? Have we become so consumed with hatred and bitterness we've become as callused as a school of sharks that turn on their own members? How can we condemn the Americans when we—"

Myoshibi's back was turned to Osato Goro. He didn't see the ringleader draw a Sterling .380 pistol from a shoulder holster and aim it at the back of his head. Osato squeezed the trigger. A flat-nosed bullet split the base of Haro's skull and drilled into his brain. The young man toppled to the ground—dead.

"All of us are expendable," Osato Goro stated simply. He returned the pistol to the leather pouch under his arm. "If the rest of you are unwilling to follow me, if you question our cause or lack the courage to continue this mission, kill me now. I would rather die than take the life of another brother. Yet I would kill all of you before I'd allow us to fail. Decide, my brothers.''

The surviving members of the Tigers of Justice bowed to their leader.

"Sore des yoi," Osato declared, humbly returning the gesture. "It is good."

Rafael Encizo shoved the gas pedal to the floor and cursed as the speedometer's needle seemed to drag across the numerals. He glanced in the rearview mirror and saw the headlights of two vehicles rapidly approaching. Even with the modified engine, the van was too large and heavy to outrun the small compact cars of the Tigers of Justice.

"In case you didn't notice," he called to his partner, "we're in trouble."

"I noticed," K.O. assured him.

"That's nice," Rafael muttered as he opened the glove compartment and extracted a Smith & Wesson Model 59.

A sturdy, double-action autoloading pistol, the S&W holds fifteen 9mm rounds in its standard magazine. After correcting various shortcomings in the earlier 59s and its Model 39 predecessor, Smith & Wesson created a formidable piece with an impressive capacity for ammunition.

Rafael placed the gun on the seat beside him and looked at the road. Suddenly two luminous eyes appeared in the distance. The headlights drew closer, but Rafael wasn't concerned about the driver's safety. The car was moving on the same side of the road as the van—heading directly toward it like a guided missile. A bullet flew from the passenger's side of the car, hitting the van's windshield.

"*Mierda!*" the Cuban growled. "The *bastardos* are trying to sandwich us in a cross fire!"

The two pursuing vehicles, a Mustang and a Volvo, continued to close in on the van. Nasaki, the harelipped Tiger of Justice, leaned out the window of the Mustang and fired a Dan Wesson .357 Magnum. He aimed at the van's rear tires, but the target's motion and the bouncing Mustang made the shot difficult. His bullet shattered a taillight and punctured the metal skin of the big machine before shooting harmlessly into the night.

Suddenly one of the rear doors of the van flew open. Nasaki and Yamato Ken, the driver of the Mustang, stared in horror at the tall figure at the door. K.O. held an M-16 in his hands. The plastic forearm grips were replaced by an M-203 grenade launcher. K.O. aimed the automatic rifle at the Mustang and fired.

A volley of copper-jacketed .223-caliber rounds slammed into the windshield. Nasaki ducked below the dashboard as the high-velocity bullets pierced the glass and chopped Yamato's face and chest into bloodied pulp. The man's corpse spun the steering wheel and the Mustang swerved off the road, skidding awkwardly into a cluster of shrubs.

If the driver of the Volvo was alarmed by the fate of the other car, it didn't influence his determination to catch up with the van. He stamped the accelerator as his passenger tried to aim a .45 Army Colt automatic at the tall Oriental who'd blasted their comrades' vehicle.

K.O. braced the M-16 against his hip and pulled the trigger of the 203. The recoil of the grenade launcher rode through the frame of the rifle like the kick of a 10-gauge shotgun. K.O. immediately jumped away from the opening as the shell found its mark. An HE loaded projectile crashed into the hood of the Volvo.

The grenade exploded on impact, bursting the car. Both terrorists in the Volvo were dead even before bits of glass and steel sliced into their flesh. The force of the explosion knocked the car backward. Sparks ignited the gasoline, blowing the tank. Another explosion sent the mangled Volvo tumbling on its side, flames spewing from the wreckage.

The last terrorist car, a Volkswagen Rabbit, continued to race toward the van. Rafael ground his teeth together and grimly accepted their challenge to play a deadly game of chicken. The passenger in the Rabbit exchanged his pistol for an M-16 and fired out the window. Bullets slapped into the van's windshield, cracking spiderweb patterns across the glass.

Rafael huddled low behind the steering wheel, but he didn't change the charge of his vehicle.

A second before the van and Rabbit collided, the terrorist driver swerved to the right. Aware the compact VW would suffer more damage than the larger vehicle, he desperately tried to avoid the big green machine. He succeeded in swinging the nose of the car out of the way, but the van smashed into the side of the Rabbit before it could roll clear.

Metal crunched and glass shattered. The violent contact sent the Tiger driver through the windshield. His torn body fell to the asphalt, bouncing across the road. Half the bones in his body were broken—including his neck and back.

Rafael stepped on the brake and the van screeched to a halt. He grabbed the M-59 as he watched a second figure emerge from the passenger's side of the crumpled Rabbit.

Hirito, the clubfooted fanatic, shook his head to clear it. Blood trickled from a gashed brow into his left eye, and his right elbow had been broken during the collision. Still, the crazy Tiger of Justice was motivated by his consuming hatred and determination to destroy the men in the van. Ignoring pain, Hirito placed his M-16 across the hood of the VW and aimed.

The terrorist yanked the trigger and blasted half a dozen rounds into the van's windshield. Glass shattered and bullets ricocheted off metal. Hirito lowered his weapon and raised his head slightly to stare at the enemy vehicle. He blinked, trying to clear his vision to see if he'd killed the driver.

Hirito never heard the sharp crack of the pistol. A 115-grain, 9mm hollowpoint bullet smashed into his forehead, executing a messy frontal lobotomy. The M-16 fell from his limp fingers, and Hirito slumped across the Rabbit's hood.

Rafael Encizo cautiously approached, the S&W in hand. He'd climbed out of the van on the passenger's side before the terrorist opened fire. The Cuban waited on the opposite side of the van until his opponent exposed himself.

In the back of the green machine, K.O. wisely elected to remain on the floor when he felt the impact with the Tiger's car and didn't rise until they came to a full halt. M-16 in hand, he moved to the rear entrance, eager to discover if they'd dispatched the last of their opponents.

He immediately found they hadn't.

Although the driver of the Mustang was dead, Nasaki's quick reflexes saved his life. The .357 Magnum popped from his grasp when the car went off the road, but he escaped uninjured. Seeing the van stop, he crept forward with the stealth of a stalking cat.

Nasaki seized K.O.'s assault rifle and jerked the startled Phoenix Force member off balance. K.O. fell from the back of the van and crashed to the ground.

He looked up to see the harelipped killer standing over him, the M-16 held by the barrel and raised overhead like a club.

"Kaii!" Hirito snarled as he swung the rifle.

K.O. rolled rapidly and the hard plastic butt of the M-16 chopped into the asphalt where his head had been. With a smooth movement the tall man sprang to his feet and assumed a T-*dachi* karate stance.

Nasaki altered his tactics and thrust the muzzle of the rifle at K.O.'s midsection, planning to follow the bayonet-style lunge with a fast butt stroke to the head. K.O. deflected the barrel as his right fist drove a *seiken* punch to Nasaki's face. He then smashed the terrorist in the mouth. Nasaki's harelip was further disfigured as broken teeth cut it like fragments of flint.

The Tiger of Justice staggered back from the blow. K.O. swiftly executed a roundhouse kick, ripping the rifle from his adversary's grasp. Moving in a circular pattern with the kick, K.O. pivoted and brought himself closer to Nasaki. The point of his elbow rammed into the terrorist's solar plexus.

Nasaki doubled over with a groan. K.O. raised his arm high and delivered another *empi* stroke, his elbow descending like a guillotine blade. The result was fatal. The blow struck Nasaki at the base of the neck, snapping the vulnerable seventh vertebra. The fanatic fell to the asphalt in a lifeless heap.

"K.O?" Rafael called out, jogging to the rear of the van. "You all right, amigo?"

The tall Japanese nodded in reply. "I'm certain none of our pursuers survived, but I wonder why the others did not join the chase."

"*Sí,*" Rafael agreed. "There were *six* cars back there. Maybe the rest drove off in another direction. They might have headed across the desert to set up another ambush between here and Phoenix. Speaking of which, we'd better contact our friends and tell them what happened."

"Yes," K.O. said. "And we must stop the Tigers of Justice from succeeding in their most ruthless mission of all—and their last."

"And we have less than twenty-four hours to find out where and what it is," Rafael added grimly.

13

Harrison Reed removed his glasses, pinched the bridge of his nose and sighed. "All this flying about the country is tiresome," he complained. "Especially when the trip turns out to be pointless."

"We don't know what information is worthless until we evaluate it, Mr. Reed," Yakov Katzenelenbogen commented. He didn't even bother to look up as he scanned a list of recent visitors at the Quinton plant.

"The situation we're faced with is critical," Professor Milton Cohen added. He and Reed were ordered to find the names of everyone who'd been at the attacked nuclear installations and to deliver the information to Phoenix Force. "I think we can tolerate a little inconvenience."

Reed scowled. "The idea that a member of the NRC would be connected with these terrorists is absurd!" He glared at Gary Manning. "I told you that on the phone, Mr. Cartwright."

The Canadian stood in the kitchenette and poured himself a cup of coffee. The group congregated in

Denver's Walgood Hotel to discuss new strategy against the Tigers of Justice. They met in Gary's room because K.O. and Rafael had Gary's phone number.

"And you're so bleeding smart you never make a mistake, eh?" David snorted, disgusted with the NRC man.

"Take it easy," Gary urged. "After all, Reed is right. We went over the lists and the only plant that was recently inspected by the NRC was the Hamel installation. The attempt there didn't require any knowledge of the plant's security systems."

The Englishman shrugged and pulled the tab off a Coke can. "Somebody has to be helping those black-suited bastards," he insisted. "Is there some sort of nuclear power plant workers' union that might connect employees of different installations together somehow?"

"Nothing like that exists," Cohen replied.

"Why were these particular plants chosen?" Yak muttered. "There has to be a connection somewhere."

"And I might have it," Gary answered, holding up two files. "There were EPA inspections at both the Janson and Hamel plants earlier this month."

"What the hell is an EPA?" David asked as he rummaged through his stack of reports.

"The Environmental Protection Agency," Cohen explained. "They check factories, chemical companies, mining operations, automobile manufacturers and almost anything else that might pollute or otherwise endanger the environment. They inspect nuclear power plants for radiation leaks or other flaws in construction.''

"EPA inspection at the Quinton plant," Yak declared. "Eight days ago."

"Janson, too," the Englishman added. "Five days ago."

"The Hamel plant's inspection was ten days ago, and the Wadsworth installation had one two days before it was hit," Gary said with a trace of excitement in his voice. "Okay. Name of the inspector?"

"Donald Grover," the Israeli replied, glancing hopefully at his partners for confirmation.

"Same at the Janson plant," David said.

"Donald Grover," the Canadian smiled. "Hamel and Wadsworth, as well."

"There's our connection," the Briton said, rubbing his palms together in expectation.

"The EPA inspection was held at Hamel first," Reed noted. "But it was the third plant to be assaulted."

"The terrorists must have considered it too risky, either because it's a breeder reactor or because security was too tight," Gary answered. "They must have decided to try dive-bombing into it after the first two attempts failed."

"But why would Grover help the Tigers of Justice?'' Reed asked lamely, well aware no one had an answer.

"We'll have Sommer pull a few strings in Washington to get the personnel records of the man,'' Yak stated. "Perhaps that will tell us something.''

"Who gives a bloody damn why he's doing it?'' David demanded. "He's helping the sons of bitches. That's all we need to know.''

"We don't know that,'' Gary said. "There's a possible connection, but that isn't definite proof.''

"It says here Grover's main office is in Los Angeles,'' the Englishman said, glancing at the report. "We'll find the evidence there.''

"Look, this isn't the sort of thing that requires a commando raid like the one you took part in...'' Yak began, stopping before he mentioned the Iranian Embassy in London. Reed and Cohen weren't supposed to know any more about Phoenix Force than necessary. "A while back. We can get the information in a more subtle manner.''

"Did Mr. Sommer return to Washington?'' Professor Cohen inquired. "I'm surprised he isn't here with us.''

"He decided to take a night flight to another state to see if Mr. Tanaka and Mr. Sanchez might need some assistance,'' Gary replied. "They're checking out another lead.''

"What lead?'' Reed snapped. "Damn it! I have a right to know—''

"Exactly what we wish to tell you," Yak interrupted, his voice as cold and hard as frozen steel. "Nothing less and nothing more."

The NRC man turned. He tried to think of something to say, but the telephone rang before he could find suitable words. Gary answered it.

"Yes," he said.

"This is Tanaka," K.O. said. "We found the headquarters of the Tigers of Justice. Osato is their ringleader."

"I see," the Canadian replied, trying to keep his tone unemotional. "If you and Mr. Sanchez need assistance, contact the Justice people at the prearranged area. Mr. S. should be there by now."

"Complications have developed," K.O. stated. "We will have to get rid of our van before we return to the city. We shall call the Justice people, but I fear the Tigers may flee their lair by then."

"Any idea where they'll go?"

"No, but they plan another unpleasant activity within the next twenty-four hours."

Gary turned to Yak and McCarter. "Get ready to move!" he said. "David, you have a valid flying license for this country, don't you?"

"Yes," the Briton replied. "And I've got a twin-engine Beech ready at the Denver airport."

"Tell 'em to get it ready. We're leaving immediately." Gary returned his attention to the phone. "Anything else, Mr. Tanaka?"

"Six of the Tigers of Justice have joined their ancestors, but others are already at their next assignment. Also, Osato spoke of an American ally. Apparently he has considerable sources of information and resources. Perhaps we should not discuss this on the phone. You do plan to join us, yes?"

"Yes, indeed," the Canadian confirmed. "Take care, Mr. Tanaka."

"Safe journey, Mr. Cartwright," K.O. replied before he hung up.

"What's going on?" Reed demanded.

"I'm afraid I'll have to ask you gentlemen to leave," Gary replied, looking up a phone number. "I'm calling Sommer about some confidential matters."

"Jesus," the NRC man fumed. "This is outrageous to be left in the dark when a nuclear catastrophe might be in progress!"

"Now you know how the general public feels when you fellas cover up the truth," Gary replied coyly.

"Mr. Cartwright," Cohen began in a gentle voice, "perhaps we should join you."

"If we need you, you'll be contacted," Yak assured him, feeling sorry for the little NRDA scientist. He was being cut out of the adventure, and he didn't want to be.

"Will we be informed of the outcome?" Cohen asked hopefully.

"The curtain is rising on the final act," the Canadian told him. "If it turns out to be a happily-ever-after ending, we'll let you know. If it doesn't—well, the whole world will probably know."

"That is," David added, "everyone who survives."

Wade Sommer unsheathed his snub-nose .38 Colt revolver from a shoulder holster. He gazed at the sun as though surprised to find it. In fact, he had never drawn the weapon except on a firing range. Shoot-'em-up encounters were the sort of thing he saw on television. How would he react if a real gun battle erupted that night?

Although Mr. Tanaka and Mr. Sanchez said they suspected the Tigers of Justice had already left the farmhouse, there was no guarantee the terrorists wouldn't be waiting for them. Hell! Half a dozen fanatics chased the antiterrorist hotshots ten miles and opened up with pistols and automatic weapons! What other surprises did the bastards have?

Of course, the tall Oriental and the Latino had killed the Tigers when they caught the Phoenix Force van. Their bodies were shot up, blown to pieces and one had a broken neck. Yeah, those five dudes were tough. Sommer found comfort in the fact one of them sat beside him in the back of the car as he and two other Justice Department agents sped down the graveyard-quiet road.

Sommer turned to look at Keio Ohara. The big

Japanese was calmly loading a thirty-round magazine into the well of his M-16 rifle. He then inserted a cartridge grenade into the breech of the 203 attachment. Damn, what a combination weapon! If you can't shoot 'em up, blow 'em up. The antiterrorists were ruthless sons of bitches. . . .

But so were the Tigers of Justice.

"We will soon approach the farmhouse," K.O. announced.

"Did I tell you your buddies called me even before you did?" Wade Sommer asked nervously. "I've got Washington looking into the records of a guy in the EPA who might be connected with the terrorists. Did I mention the other three members of your team are flying out here, too?"

"Yes," the Japanese replied patiently. "That is why Mr. Sanchez returned to Phoenix, to meet them at the airport."

"Yeah," the Justice man nodded, embarrassed by his display of jitters.

"I see it now, Mr. Sommer," the driver, a young agent named McNally, declared. "Should we get out and go the rest of the way on foot?"

"Well. . . ." The special investigator wished somebody would take the responsibility off his shoulders. He was a desk jockey, not a goddamn soldier. "You and Jones stay with the car and get those Thompsons out of the trunk. You cover Mr. Tanaka and me while we approach the house."

"Okay, sir," McNally replied as he applied the brakes.

The driver killed the headlights and the four men emerged from the car. They parked close enough to see the house clearly. At least one light was still on inside the dwelling, although no cars remained. Apparently the terrorists had fled.

"How do you want to work this, Tanaka?" Sommer asked, trying to hide his nervousness.

"Since my weapon has greater range and destructive capability, I will go first," K.O. explained, recognizing Sommer's apprehension and supplying a reason for assuming the dangerous role of point man. "If nothing happens, I should reach the house unmolested. I will move to the side and look through the windows. If it is clear, I'll call you to join me. Is this plan satisfactory?"

"Yeah, I guess so," Sommer replied.

K.O. moved forward cautiously, his M-16 held ready. Although he felt ninety-nine percent certain the house was empty, he still treated the task with the same care he used earlier that night. Drawing closer, he detected no movement at the windows and heard no sound of life from within. Slowly he crept to the west side of the building.

Wade Sommer felt foolish standing between the house and the car. The Jap was taking all the risks. How old was this Tanaka? Twenty-five, twenty-six, not much more than that. A goddamn kid giving him orders. What was he supposed to do if anything happened? Provide cover with a short-barreled .38 that lost accuracy and power if the range exceeded thirty feet?

He glanced back at McNally and Jones. The two men were positioned behind the car, the barrels of their big Thompson choppers jutting above the hood like two metal spikes. They knew Sommer was scared, and they knew that overgrown gook was really in charge. Screw all of them, Sommer thought angrily. He'd show the bastards he wasn't afraid and he wouldn't be treated like a goddamn rookie who had to get instructions to blow his nose.

Wade Sommer arrogantly strode toward the house.

K.O. eased his back along the wall and carefully peered around the edge of the window frame. He saw furniture, a fireplace and a few discarded soft-drink cans, but no occupants. The Tigers of Justice were gone.

Wade gasped when he nearly tripped over the corpse of Myoshibi Haro at the base of the front steps. Christ, the smart-ass antiterrorists hadn't mentioned there was a stiff lying in front of the place. Maybe they didn't know. The Justice man stared down at the red smear that covered the back of the dead man's skull. He felt his stomach threaten to disgorge. Then he caught his breath and continued to march stubbornly to the house.

K.O. surveyed the room. There were cold ashes in the fireplace and a poker near the hearth. It appeared the terrorists burned something before they left. His gaze turned to the front door. K.O.'s eyes widened when he saw the thick black wire wrapped around the knob. The cord extended to a glob of puttylike substance lodged in the crack of the door.

Then K.O. heard the thump-thump of footsteps on the porch. Quickly he turned and rushed toward the front of the house.

"Don't touch the door!" he shouted.

Wade Sommer had already turned the knob before he heard the Phoenix Force professional's voice. The pressure-operated detonator imbedded in the C-4 plastic explosive ignited the booby trap. A violent blast transformed the door into a spray of splinters and shattered glass and framework from the windows.

The fierce bellow of the explosion ringing in his ears, K.O. hurled himself to the ground as debris pelted his prone form. A mangled bloodied object fell near his head. He looked up to see the remains of Wade Sommer's severed arm.

14

Gary Manning inspected the smoldering remains of
the farmhouse by the pale light of dawn. The explosion shattered the front of the building and shook the
entire structure, breaking second-story windows.
McNally, one of the young Justice agents, joined the
Canadian.

"The house belonged to a farmer named Benson,"
he explained. "The guy took his family on a camping
trip for the weekend. Jesus, will he have an unpleasant surprise when he gets back!"

"He's lucky he didn't come home early," Gary
replied in a toneless voice. "These terrorists have less
regard for human life than you or I have for cock-
roaches."

"Too bad about Mr. Sommer," McNally said
awkwardly. "He just touched that door and bang!
The explosion blew him to bits. It was awful."

"Mr. Tanaka warned Sommer to stay back until
he was told it was safe to move forward," the Canadian stated simply. "He should have listened."

"Yeah," the Justice agent agreed, although he

considered Mr. Cartwright's attitude extremely cold. "Lucky the Jap wasn't hurt."

"No thanks to Sommer," Gary muttered. "His John Wayne act not only cost him his life, it could have got Tanaka killed, too. Luckily the terrorists used a small charge."

"It didn't seem like such a small charge when it went off."

"The Tigers of Justice used C-4 plastic explosives," the Phoenix Force demolitions expert replied. "Believe me, they used only a couple ounces, or we'd be standing in a crater instead of a house. It was a booby trap. They set it out of cruelty, assuming the people trying to stop them would go through the door. Typical of the terrorist mentality—ruthless, vicious and cold-blooded regardless of nationality or ideology."

"What if an innocent person entered instead?" McNally wondered aloud. "Farmer Benson, for example."

"The terrorists feel their cause justifies the loss of innocent lives," Gary answered. "That's typical of their kind, as well."

He cleared a path through the rubble. A heavy wooden beam had fallen from the ceiling and blocked his path. The powerfully built Canadian pushed it aside. He reached the fireplace and knelt by the hearth to examine the ashes. Gary grunted with satisfaction as he pulled a small charred strip of brown wax paper from the fireplace.

"What is it?" McNally asked.

"Unless I'm mistaken, it's part of a wrapper for a military-issue, two-pound block of C-4," the explosives expert told him. "And I've handled enough of the stuff to have a pretty good idea what it is. From the looks of these ashes they must have burned about four or five wrappers."

"Is that a lot?"

"Eight to ten pounds," Gary said. "You saw what a couple ounces of C-4 can do. What do you think?"

"That's a lot," McNally said mechanically.

Gary emerged from the wreckage of the farmhouse and casually dusted off his Windbreaker and jeans. Yakov Katzenelenbogen and Keio Ohara stood by the big black four-door Buick the Israeli rented at the airport. Another car full of Justice Department men and two Highway Patrol cars had also arrived.

"Find anything?" Yak inquired, tossing a cigarette butt to the ground.

"Only that the Tigers of Justice have enough plastique to blow up a small city," the Canadian replied. "They burned the wrappers in the fireplace, so my guess is they've molded the stuff to fit into something for transportation reasons. C-4 is as flexible as clay. They could put it into hollow ceramic statues, inside lamps, or in any of a thousand other items."

"The second crew of Justice agents brought us a message in response to Sommer's call to Washington," Yak said.

"They checked the personnel records of Donald Grover?" Gary asked eagerly.

The Israeli nodded. "The man has a sterling reputation. He's a good provider for his wife and children, a hard worker and an honest employee. He makes a good salary as an inspector for the EPA. He has a degree in physics. So guess what he specializes in?"

"Investigating nuclear power plants." Gary shrugged. "Tell me something we didn't know."

"Here are a few interesting items," Yak said, responding to the challenge. "Donald Grover's parents died twenty years ago. He has no brothers or sisters or close relatives. He has no military background or police record. Fifteen years ago he simply left his job as a science teacher at Medsville High School, Nebraska, to move to California and join the EPA. He lost his Nebraska driver's license and got a California license—although a check failed to find any license or record of any kind in Nebraska. When the government looked into his past, they found his birth certificate was also missing."

"Fifteen years ago he leaves everybody who knows him, gets a new career with the EPA and there are no old records of his fingerprints to cross-check with the new ones or any relatives who care whether the Donald Grover in California is the same man who used to teach in Nebraska," Gary said, evaluating the information. "A perfect background for a sleeper agent."

"Exactly," Yak agreed. "Fifteen years ago someone—probably the KGB—replaced the real Donald Grover with an impostor and destroyed any evidence that might expose their man."

"This not only explains how the Tigers of Justice were able to learn a great deal about each installation," K.O. said, gingerly touching a blister he received at the nape of his neck from a burning piece of wood, "it also tells us how the Tigers were able to smuggle most of their members into the country and who has financed their activities and supplied them with arms and equipment."

"And we can guess why," Gary added. "The Soviets would be delighted to see the United States out of the nuclear power business."

"Of course, Grover—or whatever his real name is—has been responsible for the malfunctions of the security devices at the plants, as well," the Israeli added. "A KGB sleeper is taught the dirty tricks of sabotage along with being given instructions about the country he's to infiltrate."

"Yeah," Gary nodded. "A sleeper can speak the language without an accent and knows the customs and history like a native. The Russians train their special agents for years to get their Americanization down pat. Then they sneak the spy into the country and tell him to wait until they're ready to use him. The sleeper masquerades as a Yank until the orders from Moscow arrive. He often has to wait years before they give him that special assignment."

"Fifteen years in this case," Yak declared flatly.

"What do you make of the dead Tiger the terrorists left behind, K.O?" Gary inquired.

"He must have defied Osato," the tall Japanese replied. "Perhaps he realized the madness of their plan. Or he may have objected to leaving his comrades when they pursued Rafael and me. Japanese organizations of this type form strong brotherhood bonds. Osato must have executed him as an example to the others."

"You mean he murdered him," Gary corrected.

"To Osato it was an execution," K.O. insisted. "His bitterness and hatred for the United States is an obsession, and he believes his destructive goal to be just punishment for his personal suffering because of the bombing of Hiroshima."

"He's insane," the Israeli said, shaking his head.

"One should always try to understand what motivates an enemy," K.O. stated. "Even a demented enemy."

"Did you learn anything else about the terrorists from listening to their meeting last night?" Gary inquired.

"Only that most of them do not know they are affiliated with the KGB," K.O. replied. "They referred to their 'American ally.' Osato surely must know the truth. Unfortunately they did not mention the site of their next assault."

"The Justice Department has told the Highway Patrol a carefully edited version of our problem," Yak said. "The police are aware we're dealing with terrorists, although they don't know how serious the situation is. One of their helicopters followed the tracks of the three automobiles Osato and the others escaped in. The tires made a distinct trail in the sand, allowing them to track it easily by air. The cars headed west and eventually reached a road that merges with Route 10. That leads to California."

"Have they set up road checks?" Gary inquired.

"Yes," the Israeli answered. "And three cars driven by Japanese should be easy to notice. But the terrorists have a good four-hour head start, and they may have already crossed into the next state."

"Providing this isn't another modern variation of the old ninja trick to throw us off track," the Canadian remarked.

"I do not think it is," K.O. commented. "The Tigers are determined to complete their final mission, and apparently everything is planned for a specific place and time. They won't risk getting off schedule by using a diversion."

"Then they'd head for Southern California," Yak commented.

"California's a hell of a big territory," Gary mused. "And there's about half a dozen nuclear plants scattered throughout the state."

"We better leave immediately," the Israeli said.

"The Justice Department is handling the Highway Patrol, but the police might decide to question us personally about the matter, and we can't afford any delays."

"Will we be able to contact David and Rafael?" K.O. inquired.

"I've got a radio set on the frequency to reach David's Beech," Gary replied. "And Yak installed a telephone in the Buick. David has the number, so he'll be able to contact us."

"I just hope he and Rafael don't fly off the handle when they meet Grover," the senior member of Phoenix Force remarked. "Neither are exactly diplomats, especially David."

"Our British friend has a short temper," Gary agreed. "But he isn't stupid, and Rafael usually keeps his cool unless something ignites that mean streak."

"We'd better get out of here," Yak said.

"You know, you aren't supposed to take a rented vehicle across state lines," Gary remarked as they rushed to the Buick.

"How unfortunate," the Israeli replied dryly.

15

Donald Grover poured a generous portion of Jim Beam into a glass. Sometimes he had trouble recalling the days when he was known as Mikhail Ivanovich Markov or that he was a major in the Soviet *Komitet Gosudarstvennoy Bozopasnosti*.

He had trained for seven years in "Little America," near Kiev. Like many Russian officers, especially KGB operatives, Markov learned English in school before they sent him to the "Americanized" training camp. But then he was taught to speak it without a Slavic accent.

Speaking English was only part of the intensive program. He read only American magazines and books, saw only American movies, ate American food and smoked American cigarettes. Markov lived in an environment manufactured by the KGB to be as American as possible. He often found himself enjoying the artificial U.S. culture, but General Liesko's instructors were always present to remind Markov and the other students that capitalism was decadent and the Americans were enemies of Russia.

However, Liesko's staff wasn't with him for the past fifteen years. Donald Grover discovered real American society quite different from what he was taught in the USSR. Grover learned to appreciate the free enterprise system that allowed a man to earn a living. He could advance not because a political party gave him the privilege but by his own efforts. People in the United States criticized their government without fear of punishment; they owned cars and homes, and even the poorest Americans lived better than most Soviet citizens.

Donald Grover enjoyed being American. He didn't want to return to the USSR. Grover was married to an American woman, and his two daughters were born in a Los Angeles hospital. He had a fine home in a good area and drove a handsome car.

But occasionally representatives from the Kremlin contacted him. They asked about his progress, issued orders and, no doubt, checked his activities. Donald Grover would never be free of the KGB. He considered defecting. Yet he knew the efficiency of the Russian organization. SMERSH assassins could strike anywhere, at any time—and they were ruthless enough to punish Grover's wife and children, also.

So Donald Grover—Major Mikhail Ivanovich Markov—remained "loyal" to Russia. He had no choice.

As he sat behind his desk at the Los Angeles section of the Environmental Protection Agency, he grimly considered his orders. The plan to use the Tigers of Justice to disrupt the American nuclear program was less successful than anticipated. The original plan of making the incidents look like accidents had failed. Although the U.S. government still covered the truth from the general public, federal agencies were aware terrorists were responsible, and it was only a matter of time before the Japanese fanatics would be apprehended.

Moscow, however, still hoped to accomplish its primary goal. One final target remained for the Tigers of Justice. This time they had to succeed. Grover would accompany them to be sure they did. After the reactor meltdown occurred, the terrorists would be on their own. Without aid from their "American ally" they would be unable to leave the country. They would soon be seized by the police or the feds, unless they chose to commit suicide—which would serve the same purpose. Osato Goro and Sakata Fujo were the only members of the organization who knew the KGB was involved. SMERSH would deal with them.

Donald Grover's cover would be burned by his participation in the terrorist mission. The KGB would smuggle him out of the country, back to the Soviet Union. He was told the Kremlin would reward him for his years of service and a promotion would be waiting when he returned....

Home. Home was with Norma and the kids. Home

was Los Angeles with its smog, traffic and all the rest. Home was America. The bitter irony of the situation cut into Grover's heart like a cold razor blade. He was going to help destroy the nation he loved because the land of his birth—which he'd grown to hate—ordered him to.

No, he thought. Russia isn't to blame. The people of the Soviet Union aren't responsible for their government, since only twelve percent belong to the Party. Even the manipulators in Moscow aren't at fault. They were raised on propaganda since the days of Lenin. No one is to blame and no one can stop the horror that will be unleashed before this day ends.

His thoughts were interrupted when Carla Michaels, his secretary, entered the office. A pert pretty blonde with a pleasant personality and all the idealistic optimism of youth, she regarded her boss as the champion defender of American's environment. How would she react if she knew Donald Grover was actually a Russian spy? Hell, Carla wouldn't believe it if he showed her a hammer-and-sickle tattoo next to his heart.

"There's a gentleman to see you, Mr. Grover," she announced. The gleam in Carla's blue eyes and the upward curl at the corners of her mouth told Grover she found the visitor attractive.

"I'm very busy, Carla," he told her. "And I have a plant to inspect this afternoon."

"But he's come all the way from England, Mr.

Grover,'' the secretary said. "He's a member of the British Safety Commission, and he wants to talk to you about nuclear power plants.''

Christ, you'd think this guy was Prince Charles, Grover thought. "All right, Carla. I'll see him, but only for a few minutes.''

"Yes, sir,'' she replied, almost skipping from the room.

Half a minute later a tall man with long sideburns, a neat mustache and a rumpled powder-blue shirt entered the office. Grover rose from his chair and extended a hand.

"Mr. Grover?'' David McCarter inquired.

Who the hell else would be here? Grover thought, but said, "That's right, Mr.—?''

"Masters,'' the Briton replied as they shook hands. "Eugene Masters.''

"Please be seated,'' Grover said, sinking back in his chair. "What can I do for you, Mr. Masters?''

"Well, I'm a safety inspector in my country,'' David began. "Similar job to yours.''

"I'm EPA, not OSHA.''

"Ah, but you're an authority on nuclear power plants, and that's what I need. You see, I'm supposed to return to England and start mucking about those devilish installations to see what's what,'' he said, smiling sheepishly. "And frankly, I haven't the foggiest notion what to look for.''

"Mr. Masters,'' Grover sighed. "I can't give you a

crash course in physics. I've got an appointment."

"My country's planning to construct a new breeder reactor to produce more plutonium so we won't have to import it from you chaps."

"What kind of breeder?" Grover asked.

"A Fermi reactor, it's called."

"Jesus." The EPA man shook his head. "They aren't thinking of using a liquid-sodium coolant system, are they?"

"I really don't know."

"Better find out," Grover said. "And if they are, discourage it. Liquid sodium transfers heat well and it prevents reactor rods from melting in intense temperature, perhaps a thousand degrees or higher. It also allows for lower pressure levels within the reactor vessel. However, sodium is a very touchy and deadly substance. If exposed to water or even air, it will explode. Sodium absorbs radiation at a much greater degree than water. If there's a leak in the coolant system, you've got a highly unstable and dangerous element that makes nitroglycerin look like tap water."

"My God," David said, raising his eyebrows in alarm. "I must say, that doesn't sound very safe at all, does it? I'll have to have a chat with my superiors about this when I get back home."

"That's a good idea, Mr. Masters," Grover agreed. "But I'm really very busy. If you'll excuse me...."

Without warning an outrageous figure burst into the office. A stocky Latino dressed in Levi's and boots with an unbuttoned, sleeveless denim jacket stomped forward, waving a small Puerto Rican flag at the end of a long pole with a crude point.

"Free Puerto Rico!" Rafael cried, brandishing the flagpole like a spear.

David leaped from his chair and dashed behind Grover's desk to avoid the slashing lance. "Bloody lunatic!" he exclaimed.

"I'm sorry, Mr. Grover," Carla declared fearfully as she appeared at the door. "He just walked in and...."

"Call security," the EPA man snapped, his eyes never leaving the absurd yet menacing figure in the center of the room.

"You gringos forced American citizenship on my country," Rafael snarled. "You try t'make Puerto Rico the fifty-first state and all that crap. Now you gonna try to build a mess of nuclear plants there, too. We don't want you Yankee *bastardos* in Puerto Rico. We don't want you makin' our country into no Three Mile Island."

"I'm an inspector for the Environmental Protection Agency," Grover told him in a patient voice. "Why don't you tell the NRC your complaints, young man?"

"You poke around in nuclear plants, no?" Rafael replied, his eyes bulging fiercely. "You one of them atomic guys. Don't jive me! We ain't messin' around with you guys no more.''

David McCarter took advantage of the distraction to examine the clipboard on Donald Grover's desk. An inspection form was attached to it. The English-man read: "NUCL. POW. PLT, MARSTON.''

"Look, you'd better leave, fella,'' Grover declared, glancing at his watch. "The police will be here soon.''

"I go all right,'' the Cuban snorted. "But you remember what I tell you, gringo!''

He turned and bolted from the room. Rafael ran through Carla's office and into the corridor. Two uniformed guards ran toward him until Rafael swung the point of his flagpole at them. Both stopped. One reached for his side arm, but Rafael stepped forward and cracked the lance across the guard's wrist. The revolver fell from his fingers.

The other security man made his move, trying to grab the "PR nut.'' Rafael turned and jabbed the blunt end of his pole into the man's solar plexus. The guard gasped in breathless agony and wilted to the floor. Rafael sprinted the length of the corridor to the emergency fire stairs.

"Spic son of a bitch,'' the patrolman with the fractured wrist muttered as he picked up his gun with his other hand.

"I'll call the police,'' Carla announced. She rushed to the phone on her desk.

"Forget it," Grover told her, stepping from his office. "I have an appointment at the Marston plant at two and I don't want to have to waste time answering questions about that idiot. He's gone, that's all that matters."

"Well," David chuckled nervously. "A bit of excitement there, eh?"

"I apologize for this, Mr. Masters," the EPA man said. "It's never happened before. But I suppose everyone is a bit emotional about these nuclear accidents lately. They're all looking for someone to blame."

"Not your fault," the Englishman assured him.

"I really must be going now," Grover explained. "I hope you have a safe trip back to England, and I'm sorry I wasn't able to be of more help."

"On the contrary," David replied with a grin. "I learned just about everything I hoped to. Have a good day."

16

Osato Goro warmed with the satisfaction and thrill of participating in the Tigers of Justice's final mission. The terrorist leader smiled when the truck approached the Marston Nuclear Power Plant. Nothing would go wrong this time, he thought. Judgment Day for the United States of America had arrived.

The Marston plant was located on the outskirts of Marston County, less than a hundred miles from San Bernadino. Unlike most atomic installations, it did not feature the familiar silos with a great dinosaur egg in the middle. Six huge metallic generators formed a column behind an enormous structure of concrete and steel. The building contained the offices, the control rooms and recycling vats for reprocessing nuclear wastes. The vessel for the reactor was installed underground, and the rest of the plant was constructed around it. The awesome uranium furnace was in the basement of the installation.

Sakata Fujo drove the truck, his expression grim with determination. The fanatic's fiery hatred of Americans even surpassed Osato's. He did not fear death, and if it was his karma that he perish, so be it. Sakata hoped to survive to see the suffering that would follow and to enjoy his revenge.

Donald Grover rode in the truck's cab with the two terrorist commanders and tried to ready himself for the task that fate cruelly thrust upon him. Despite his personal beliefs and desires, he remained a Soviet agent. He had a duty to his country, regardless of its politics. Perhaps he'd judged the USSR too harshly. After the United States terminated its nuclear program, the Russian government might do likewise as a goodwill gesture. Maybe a worldwide nuclear ban could be accomplished....

Bullshit, Grover thought. He was going to help the Japanese madmen sabotage the Marston plant because he feared the KGB too much to do otherwise.

The truck approached the fence that surrounded the installation. Two uniformed figures emerged from a guard shack and walked to the gate. Osato and Sakata tugged baseball caps low to conceal Oriental features. The truck stopped, and Grover climbed from the cab.

"I'm the EPA inspector," he announced, showing the guards his credentials and NRC pass.

"We were told to expect you, sir," a patrolman said. "What's in the truck?"

"A new antiradiation shield for the confinement section," Grover replied. "It's a titanium alloy NASA came up with. They'll be using it in the construction of reactor vessels as well as spacecraft."

"Mr. Haney didn't mention that, sir," the patrolman said. "I'll have to call to get authorization."

"May I speak to him, too?"

"Sure, Mr. Grover."

The senior guard entered the shack while his partner casually watched the truck. With a clatter of metal and steel cord, the electrically controlled gate opened to allow Grover to enter. He strolled into the shack as the patrolman placed a telephone receiver to his ear and prepared to dial. The KGB sleeper agent removed his "cigarette lighter" from his pocket.

Grinding his teeth together, Grover raised the weapon and pushed it behind the left ear of the unsuspecting security guard. He flicked the wheel, operating the firing mechanism. A small steel dart slit the patrolman's head. He felt incredible pain for less than a second, then died.

Hands trembling, Grover pushed a button and the gate opened to admit the vehicle. Sakata drove the truck inside and opened the door. The other guard stepped forward.

"May I see your identification, sir?" he asked.

Sakata reached out and seized the man by the throat. Before the startled guard could react, the Japanese karate expert's other hand swung like the blade of an axe, the edge striking the patrolman's temple. The blow cracked his skull and ruptured his brain. Sakata and Osato dragged the corpse onto the truck. Grover closed the gate and climbed into the rig.

They drove to the main building. Two more guards were stationed at the structure's shatterproof glass door. Grover's ID again gained him entry. The captain of the security force, a heavyset retired navy man, recognized the EPA inspector from previous visits.

"I don't recall you making deliveries before, Mr. Grover," he commented.

"That new shielding material is worth a fortune," the sleeper agent answered, "so they wanted me to be certain it's in the right hands."

"Mind if Mike takes a look in the back?" the captain asked.

"Of course not," Grover forced a smile. "You can't be too careful when the security of a nuclear power plant is involved."

Sakata had already unlatched one of the rear doors of the big rig. Mike, a young lanky guard, strolled to the truck as the Japanese opened it. He stared inside to see a figure dressed entirely in black with a short sword in his gloved hands. Mike's mouth fell open in astonishment a second before the blade of the *wakizashi* slashed the side of his neck, severing his jugular with a single stroke.

The guard captain saw his buddy's body crumple to the ground, blood spilling from his wound. He clawed at the .38 Colt revolver on his hip, momentarily forgetting Donald Grover, who stood behind him. Grover wrapped an arm around the captain's throat, pressed the "lighter" against the side of his head and fired a poison dart into his brain.

Twelve Tigers of Justice—some dressed in traditional ninja clothing, others clad in white laboratory smocks—emerged from the back of the truck. Barking orders, Sakata detailed two men to guard the gate. Armed with M-76 Smith & Wesson 9mm machine pistols, the pair bowed quickly and dashed to their post. Osato Goro joined Grover inside the building.

"Have we dealt with all the security personnel?" he asked, attaching a seven-inch silencer to the muzzle of his Sterling automatic.

"There are more inside," the EPA-KGB man answered. "Guards are posted at the control rooms, the waste-recycling section and the elevator to the containment area."

"That's where the pumps to the coolant system are located, yes?"

"The main pumps," Grover replied. "The emergency equipment is located in the west wing."

"I remember," Osato said. "All we need to do is destroy the main control panel and the emergency generators, and the plant is helpless to stop the meltdown. Fate favors our mission today, Major. Did you hear the weather report? This afternoon will be pleasantly cool for Southern California because a strong breeze will be coming from the north. The wind will carry radioactive fallout across San Francisco and Los Angeles to San Diego. Think of the destruction!''

"Let's get it over with," Grover said grimly.

The black Buick sped along the desolate road, often passing slower moving traffic. Since no other vehicles were travelling at ninety miles per hour, the Buick did a lot of passing and sometimes nearly ran head-on into cars coming from the opposite direction.

"My God, K.O.!" Yakov exclaimed. "Must you be so reckless?"

"I said I would get us to our destination fast, yes?" the Japanese replied, an impish grin tugging at his lips.

"We'll have a hell of a time trying to explain all this weaponry if the police stop us," the Israeli declared.

He adjusted the hooks at the end of his prosthetic arm. Three curved blades of stainless steel, they were more functional than the "hand" because Yak could operate them faster. Although the device did not include a built-in .22 Magnum, the Uzi 9mm machine pistol in his lap and the .45 Colt Commander on his hip would supply Yak with all the firepower he was apt to need.

"We lost the police half a mile ago," Gary Manning commented as he shoved an HE round into the breech of the 203 grenade launcher attached to the M-16 assault rifle. "I just hope we don't run into any roadblocks."

"We'll get through them," Keio Ohara said cheerfully.

"That's what I'm afraid of," the Canadian commented, setting the M-16 aside to check the loads of his Colt Python. He kept busy to conceal his nervousness over K.O.'s driving.

The Buick drew closer to the rear of a tractor-trailer rig. A cement truck lumbered down the opposite side of the double line. K.O. solved the problem by swerving to the right, driving off the road and smashing through a guardrail. He sped around the obstacle and shattered another rail, swinging back on the road.

"Lord help us!" Yak whispered, his eyes shut.

"I thought only flying bothered you," Gary remarked.

"This is flying," the Israeli replied. "And we've got our own kamikaze pilot at the wheel!"

"Ground team, this is Mixmaster. Over," David McCarter said on the dashboard radio.

Gary reached over from the back seat and picked up the microphone. "We read you, Mixmaster. Over."

"Glad you kept the radio on as I requested.

Over,'' the Englishman stated. He had called the other members of Phoenix Force on the car phone Yak installed and told them Donald Grover was heading for the Marston plant.

"We should be nearing our destination. Over," the Canadian said.

"I know," David chuckled. "Do you know where I am? Over."

Gary knitted his eyebrows. "Since you're using the radio, I assume you're in your plane. Over."

"That's right," the Briton answered. "And I'm flying over your vehicle. Over."

Gary glanced out the window and saw the twin-engine Beech tracking the Buick at six hundred feet. "How did you recognize the car? Over."

"I can tell by the driver. Over."

"Uh-huh," the Canadian grunted. "What are you planning to do? Over."

"Join you at our destination. Over."

"Jesus," Gary muttered. "Where do you intend to land? Over."

"I'll find a place when we get there," David assured him. "Over and out."

"Mixmaster?" Gary snapped urgently. "Mixmaster?" He turned off the microphone. "Hellfire."

"Two kamikaze pilots!" Yak said rolling his eyes in exasperation.

"There's the plant," K.O. declared, turning off the road.

The Buick charged up the long driveway that divided the spacious lawn surrounding the Marston installation. Two black-clad figures emerged from the guard shack. K.O. saw the machine pistols in their hands a split second before the terrorists opened fire. . . .

17

Gravel spewed from the ground like small geysers of hailstones. The Tigers of Justice used their weapons too soon, firing before the Buick was within machine-pistol range. K.O. stomped on the brake, bringing the car to a bone-jarring halt. The back doors popped open. Gary and Yak hopped out, using the doors as shields as they fired at the terrorists.

Gary snapped a quick burst from the M-16, the .223-caliber projectiles singing harshly as they ricocheted on the frame of the fence. The volley encouraged the ninja pair to retreat to the guard shack. Yak's Uzi barked briefly, although he realized his machine pistol was as ineffective at two hundred feet as the Tigers' M-76 chatterguns. Still, it helped pin them down, giving Gary the precious seconds he needed.

The Canadian knelt and placed the stock of the M-16 on the ground. He judged the distance to the shack and slightly altered the assault rifle. Gary pulled the trigger on the grenade launcher. The M-203 belched and discharged its HE projectile. The shell traveled in a high arc and came down squarely on the roof of the guard shack.

The tiny structure burst into a collage of twisted metal, littering fragments of glass and chips of plastic. Two mangled bodies hurtled from the wreckage and fell lifeless to the ground. The explosion broke the framework of the gate. Gary nodded with satisfaction when he saw the barrier droop from the edge of the fence.

"Do you think you can get through the door, now that it's open a crack?" he asked as he climbed back into the Buick. Yak followed his example.

"Most certainly," Keio Ohara replied, stomping on the gas pedal.

The black car roared forward and crashed into the lopsided gate like a metallic rhinoceros. Steel and wire snapped on impact, and the gate bounced aside as the Buick sped across the threshold.

"I see our friends got inside," Rafael Encizo commented. He and David McCarter watched the scene from the Beech airplane that soared above the Marston plant. "But how do we manage to do likewise?"

"Anything K.O. can do with a car," the Englishman replied, pushing the stick to the Beech's instrument panel, "I can do with a plane."

The Beech swung toward the ground at the edge of the driveway. Rafael stared in disbelief as the earth leaped up at them. *Cristo,* he thought. That's a skinny gravel path, not a runway! "I don't think this is such a good idea," the Cuban said, keeping his voice steady.

"Maybe not," the Englishman admitted. "But we're doing it anyway."

The wheels touched down. Gravel spat wildly and pelted the belly of the plane like machine-gun bullets. Rafael shook his head and wondered if everybody in Phoenix Force—including him—was a little loco. Probably, he quickly decided.

David killed the power, and the Beech rolled toward the gap in the fence. He realized the driveway wasn't long enough, but he couldn't stop the plane before it reached the fence. He couldn't take off again, either.

"If you get us killed, I'll be very unhappy," Rafael muttered through clenched teeth as the Beech rolled closer.

"Hang on," David yelled gamely. "McCarter's coming through!"

The nose of the plane entered the plant, its propellers whirling like crazed windmills. The gate wasn't wide enough for the wings. Metal crunched against metal. The plane violently vibrated as the Beech's skin ripped at the wing's sockets. David cut the engine. The Beech trembled for a moment—then nothing moved except the decelerating propellers.

"There," the Briton declared, trying to sound more relaxed than he felt. "Nothing to it."

"Next time I'll take a bus," Rafael remarked with a sigh of relief.

Osato Goro, Donald Grover, Sakata Fujo and six Tigers of Justice seized the main control room of the Marston plant. Grover's EPA and NRC documents convinced the guard to admit the "inspection team." A poison dart in the hollow of his throat told the security man he had made a serious mistake—his last. The terrorists swarmed into the room. Another guard was quickly cut down by a volley of M-76 lead. The invaders ordered the startled technicians, supervisor and chief engineer to back away from the panels. Kikomi Toshi, the group's top demolitions man, knelt by the controls and attached a large magnetic mine. He smiled as he adjusted pressure-sensitive wires to the detonator and attached them to the machine with small magnets.

"It is done," he said. "When the timer is set, it is impossible to stop the bomb. If anyone attempts to move the mine or tries to deactivate it, it will explode immediately. I have not set the timing mechanism. That honor rightfully belongs to you, Osato-sama."

"*Arigato*, Kikomi-san," the terrorist leader replied with genuine appreciation. "You have done well."

"Let us kill these bastards and be gone," Sakato Fujo urged, gesturing at the plant employees with a Walther P-38.

"We shall wait a few minutes to be certain our

brothers have had time to destroy the emergency equipment, as well.''

The sudden wail of sirens startled terrorist and Marston employee alike. Several Tigers of Justice glared at their captives, suspecting the technicians had somehow triggered the alarm. Osato turned to Donald Grover.

''What caused this?'' he asked.

''I don't know,'' Grover admitted. ''There are security alarms built into the fence and the building's exterior, but they shouldn't go off unless someone attempted forced entry.''

''The police?''

''Perhaps,'' the sleeper replied. ''Or someone may have pressed a button. There are other workers in this plant besides the eight we have here.''

''We can't take any chances,'' Osato declared. He moved to the RDX mine and turned the dial of the timing mechanism. ''If the authorities have come, they shall not leave this installation alive.''

''What did you do, Osato?'' Grover demanded, his eyes wide with fear.

''The bomb will explode in five minutes,'' the fanatic said calmly.

''You idiot!'' Grover shouted. ''Stop that thing! Reset the detonator! Do something!''

''Nothing can stop it,'' Osato smiled. ''The reactor meltdown is now irreversible. Our fate and the fate of this plant are decided.''

Another grenade blasted the door of the building apart. Even shatterproof glass isn't designed to withstand a heavy explosive round from an M-203. Keio Ohara, armed with an M-10 Ingram machine pistol, sprinted to the entrance, followed by Gary Manning and Yakov Katzenelenbogen. David McCarter and Rafael Encizo brought up the rear—both carried Ingrams and their personal weapons.

A volley of 9mm projectiles smashed into the framework of the wrecked door, forcing K.O. to leap aside. The ninja-clad Tiger of Justice stationed in the corridor held his finger on the trigger of his M-76 too long and exhausted the ammunition. While he tried to replace the spent magazine, Yak cut him down with a burst of Uzi bullets.

Phoenix Force charged into the building, their weapons held ready. A terrorist dressed in a laboratory smock was positioned at the control-room door. He barely saw the five-man team in time to raise his machine pistol. A three-round burst of .223 bullets split his face before he could use the weapon.

Gary advanced quickly and thrust the smoking muzzle of his M-16 around the door frame's edge. He peered into the room. The terrorists and their captives both wore identical white coats. The Canadian held his fire, unable to tell them apart. A Tiger squeezed off two shots with a pistol. Bullets ricocheted off the steel rim of the entrance. Gary withdrew immediately.

Recovering from the shock of the "cavalry's" arriving, the Marston employees took advantage of the unexpected distraction. Many of them had served on submarines in the navy and had seen combat in Vietnam. One man grabbed Sakata Fujo's wrist and twisted the Walther P-38 from his grasp. The karate expert slammed a forward elbow stroke to the technician's temple, knocking him to the floor. Another employee wrestled with a terrorist for possession of his weapon until a Tiger shot the operator in the back. The rest chose the safest policy in a firefight: if you don't have a gun—get down and stay down!

It was fortunate they did, because Rafael appeared at the door with his M-10. He didn't hesitate. A rapid spray of 9mm lead filled the room like a swarm of angry bees. Ragged bullet holes appeared in the smock of the terrorist pistolman as the multiple shots kicked his body across the room. The other Tigers dove for shelter. Rafael entered the room, his Ingram still blasting. David and K.O. followed, supplying cover fire for the Cuban.

Rafael crouched by the control panel that regulated the rods within the reactor. A pale-faced, middle-aged man with TRENT, R. printed on his ID badge had already crawled to the same position.

"Whoever you are," he gasped, "thank God you're here!"

"I'm glad God let us get here in time," the Cuban replied earnestly, trying to locate the remaining terrorists without exposing himself. "We killed three of them outside. Are there any left outside this room?"

"They said another team is going to sabotage the emergency generators in the west wing," Trent answered.

Rafael shouted the information to Gary and Yak, who were still in the corridor.

"I'll take care of them," the Israeli told Gary. "You are needed here."

"None of these *bastardos* will get away," Rafael assured Trent.

The engineer's expression revealed terror as he remembered the bomb Osato set to blow up the main control panel. "*None* of us will get out of here alive," he said grimly.

18

Yakov Katzenelenbogen ran down the corridor to the west wing, silently vowing to give up cigarettes and lose some weight. The Israeli turned a corner and literally ran into two terrorists dressed in ninja black.

One of the Tigers of Justice tried to use his M-76 machine pistol, but Yak's Uzi fired first. Four 9mm rounds burned through the ninja's chest like a column of smoke. The impact sent the terrorist's body sprawling across the floor.

Before the senior member of Phoenix Force could deal with the other terrorist, a streak of steel appeared in the man's hand. The ninja's *wakizashi* flashed. The blade struck the frame of the Uzi. Metal clanged, and the gun popped from the Israeli's fingers.

Yak leaped back, his reflexes overcoming his shock at finding himself face to face with an opponent armed with a samurai short sword. The terrorist raised the *wakizashi* in a two-handed grip, intent on cutting the Israeli in two with his next stroke. Yak moved close to a wall. There wasn't enough room to dodge the blade, and there wasn't enough time to reach for his Colt Commander.

Moving with remarkable speed for a man his age and size, Yak leaped forward and raised his left arm. The heel of his palm met the base of the sword handle. Yak locked his right leg, forming a solid barrier with his body and outstretched arm. The ninja could not complete the stroke.

Quickly Yak's prosthetic arm rose, the trio of steel hooks opening like metal jaws. He thrust the artificial hand under the terrorist's chin. The hook closed. Blood gushed over the ninja's black shirt as Yak ripped his throat open.

The roar of an explosion echoed from the corridor. A violent tremor moved through the structure, threatening to rattle the walls apart. Yak stared down at the dead men and shook his head. He was too late to stop the sabotage team. Their survival—and the survival of hundreds of thousands of Americans—was now in the hands of his fellow Phoenix Force members.

"Our brothers have destroyed the emergency equipment," Osato Goro said, smiling as he felt the building convulse. The terrorist leader, Sakata Fujo and Kikomi Toshi were behind the wide frame of an IBM computer panel.

"We may live to strike another blow against the Americans," Sakata replied. He pointed to a metal door across the room. "That exit beckons us," the second-in-command declared, appealing to his leader's notions of destiny. "It is our karma to find what waits beyond it."

"So be it," Osato agreed.

The three terrorists half crawled, half ran to the door. Thanks to the efforts of the remaining pair of Tiger terrorists, who exchanged shots with Phoenix Force, they reached the door. The ringleader opened the door and slipped through the exit. Sakata joined him, but Kikomi's karma spat on him. Keio Ohara stitched the Japanese demolitions expert from kidney to shoulder blade with a burst of M-10 lead missiles. Kikomi Toshi crumpled to the floor, his body lodged between the door and its frame.

Another Tiger of Justice rose from his shelter behind a printout machine and tried to blast K.O. with a .45 automatic. He exposed his head and shoulders long enough for Gary Manning to obliterate his face with a burst of M-16 bullets.

Donald Grover and the last member of the Tigers of Justice knelt behind the base of a radiation meter. If the feds—or whoever the guys with the chatterguns were—didn't get him, the reactor meltdown would. He sneered as he watched Osato and Sakata slip through the metal door. The KGB agent knew the Marston plant better than the terrorists. They had entered the boiler room, an area that contained pipes and electrical cables used to power the control room and a single flight of stairs leading down to the elevator to the containment area. There was no escape from there.

Grover knew, however, one slim chance for survival remained. Another door led to the radiation dressing room. When the bomb on the instrument panel went off, all means of stopping the meltdown would be gone. However, the uranium furnace wouldn't burn itself out immediately. If Grover could don protective clothing and a Scotch-mask helmet with oxygen tanks, he might be able to live through the radioactive fallout and escape before the actual meltdown occurred.

One chance in a million—but it was all he had. First he needed to distract the Phoenix Force commandos. He shoved the Japanese fanatic beside him into the open. The Tiger fell on his side and stared up into the flaming muzzle of David McCarter's M-10 an instant before it chopped his heart and lungs to pieces.

Grover made his move and dashed to the dressing room, turning the doorknob and diving inside. The Englishman was already running after him.

"You aren't going anywhere, you bastard!" David snarled, discarding his empty Ingram to draw the Browning hi-power pistol from a shoulder holster.

He kicked the door hard, slamming it into Grover before the sleeper could lock it. Grover staggered backward, dazed and startled—but he held his deadly "lighter" in his fist. The black muzzle of the Briton's handgun rose to face him.

"If you're trying to find the men's room," David remarked, "we can look for it together."

Grover glanced about at the heavy thick garments that hung from the ceiling like sides of beef in a slaughterhouse. The protective gear was his last hope. His hand tightened around the lighter.

"Listen," he began. "We're going to have a nuclear meltdown in about three minutes!"

"And you wanted to change your clothes to have a formal funeral, eh?"

"If you help me, I'll help you survive!"

"No deal," the Englishman snapped. "Come along or—"

Grover swung his arm forward, aiming the lighter at his opponent. David fired his pistol. The Browning hi-power is one of the most accurate handguns in the world, and David McCarter is an excellent marksman. A 9mm 125-grain hollowpoint bullet smashed between the KGB agent's eyes before he could use his dart gun. The sleeper fell to the floor, never to wake again.

Keio Ohara dashed to the metal door in pursuit of Osato Goro and Sakata Fujo. He entered the boiler room and stepped on the metal terrace of the stairs. He heard footsteps ringing on the steel and saw two figures bounding down the steps. Numerous pipes and cables blocked his view and presented a hazard if he opened fire with the Ingram. He gave chase, leaping down three steps at a time.

A confused and frightened security guard stationed at the elevator in the containment area sighed with relief when he saw the two figures in laboratory smocks descend the stairs. He holstered his Ruger revolver and opened his mouth to ask what the hell was going on up there. . . .

The Sterling automatic in Osato Goro's fist snarled. Bullets struck the guard's chest and face. He collapsed without uttering a word. Sakata scanned the bleak room. There was no exit except the elevator with the upside-down trio of pyramids symbolizing radiation stamped on its doors.

"We're trapped," Sakata hissed.

"Osato!" a voice cried from the stairwell.

The terrorists turned to see Keio Ohara nimbly descending the metal steps, his Ingram held ready. Osato Goro raised his pistol. K.O. opened fire. Three 9mm slugs ripped into the terrorist's arm and shoulder, tearing flesh and sinew into pulp and snapping bone on contact. The impact threw the fanatic back into the elevator.

"*Haaii-yaa!*" Sakata Fujo shouted as his arm swung in a blur like the blade of a sword.

The edge of his hand chopped into K.O.'s forearm. The M-10 fell from K.O.'s numb fingers. Sakata executed a *seiken* punch to the tall man's face, knocking K.O. over the railing.

Landing nimbly on his feet, Keio Ohara whirled to face the karate-trained terrorist. Sakata assumed a T-*dachi* position, hands held like twin axes. K.O. shifted into a cat stance, his fingers open and arched.

"I should have killed you before," the terrorist spat.

"You have the opportunity to try," K.O. replied, sounding more confident than he felt. His head ached from Sakata's glancing punch, and he realized a full-powered blow would have broken his jaw.

With a *kiai* shout Sakata executed an abbreviated kick at K.O.'s groin. The Phoenix Force pro recognized the move as a feint and dodged the real attack—a high snap kick with the other leg. Sakata's movements remained fast and smooth. He suddenly drove a punch to his opponent's midsection. K.O.'s breath coughed from his lungs and his body began to fold as Sakata's hand lashed out in a deadly *shuto* chop to his temple.

The tall man blocked the stroke with his forearm. Sakata kept moving, stabbing the stiffened fingers of his other hand at K.O.'s solar plexus. An elbow blocked the *nukite* thrust, and the Phoenix Force defender slammed the heel of his palm under Sakata's jaw.

An ordinary man would have been knocked unconscious or even suffered a broken neck from the whiplash effect of the karate stroke, but Sakata merely staggered back two steps and threw a kick at his adversary. K.O. checked the kick. His foot bounced off and instantly delivered a high side kick to Sakata's face.

The terrorist's head snapped back from the blow. K.O. immediately moved in, his arm slashing in a cross-body stroke. The side of his hand struck Sakata Fujo squarely on the throat, crushing his windpipe and bursting his Adam's apple. Sakata gargled on his own blood as he stumbled backward and pawed hopelessly at his throat. Then he dropped to the floor—dead.

K.O. whirled to see the doors of the elevator slide shut. Drops of blood around the entrance left no doubt where Osato Goro had gone.

Gary Manning knelt by the bomb as Yak, David, Rafael and employees of the Marston plant tensely watched. The Canadian shook his head. The timer moved to one minute and twenty seconds.

"They said it can't be stopped," Trent remarked hopelessly.

"That's crap," Gary replied flatly. "Any bomb can be deactivated. It's just a matter of doing it right."

"Hell," the Englishman said. "Pull the bloody wires. What have we got to lose?"

"Our lives," the demolitions expert answered. "These wires are pressure sensitive. That means they have to be loosened or tightened before the detonator can be removed."

"Every bomb I've seen required tension for the firing mechanism," the Israeli commented.

"That's exactly what the fellow who set this thing wanted us to think," Gary stated.

The timer moved to fifty-eight seconds.

"Jesus," David whispered. "Do something!"

"Fifty-fifty chance," the Canadian said, inserting a tiny screwdriver into the base of the first wire. "We'll know if I guessed right in a minute."

"We don't have a minute," Rafael remarked.

"That's what I mean," Gary replied, gingerly turning the tool.

The dial clicked to forty-five seconds.

Despite the urgency of the situation, Gary didn't rush. His hands remained steady, although his heart threatened to pound itself into putty. The pulse beat at the back of his ear hammered his skull like a mallet.

"Twenty-six seconds," Trent gasped, closing his eyes in prayer.

Gary tightened the last wire and reached for the detonator. He gently touched the circular blaster in the center of the mine. The timer ticked down to less than ten seconds. Right or wrong, it was too late to change tactics.

Five seconds. . . .

He jerked the detonator from the bomb.

Nothing happened.

EPILOGUE

Keio Ohara and Gary Manning stepped into the elevator. Trent, the engineer, volunteered to accompany them. Since the containment area held the main water pumps hooked into the reactor vessel, strict precautions were observed. The three men wore protective antiradiation suits, helmets and Scotch masks.

Although Osato Goro was wounded and didn't appear to be armed, they weren't taking any chances. K.O. and Gary awkwardly carried handguns in their gloved hands.

"Is the radiation level around these pumps always risky?" Gary Manning inquired. His voice echoed within the helmet.

"It's usually higher than 100 rads," Trent replied, his voice muffled by the Scotch mask. "That's not really dangerous, but it's enough to require decontamination after exposure."

"Didn't you say 450 rads are considered lethal?" Yak inquired. K.O. and Trent reminded him of aliens from another planet.

"That's right," the engineer confirmed. "But there's no need for concern. These suits are designed to protect in up to 600 rads."

"I hate to be left out of finishing this business," David remarked.

"It's too dangerous for a bunch of us to go down together in a little elevator," Gary replied. "If Osato is delirious, he may have trouble understanding English, and K.O. can talk to him in his own language. If he's set an explosive on one of the pumps, I'm the obvious choice to handle it."

"Don't take any chances with that son of a whore," Rafael urged. "If he even thinks wrong—kill him."

The doors hummed shut. Trent turned on a Geiger counter as the elevator slowly descended. Angry static pounded from the machine.

"One hundred and ten rads," he stated. "That's unusually high for the shaft."

"Maybe Osato has already sabotaged the pumps," Gary said.

The doors opened in the containment area, and they entered a small air-lock compartment. Louder static scratched from the Geiger counter as the elevator closed.

"Three hundred rads," Trent announced. "That's too high."

"We've got to go on," Gary said, pressing the button to the air lock.

Steel doors rolled back to reveal the containment area. The room resembled a cave of metal and rivets. Five large pumps on stubby stalks stood in the center like monster insects in a nightmare. The crackle of the Geiger counter increased as they stepped forward.

"Four hundred and eighty rads," Trent said, his voice revealing alarm.

Something splashed under their booted feet. "That explains it," he said, glancing at the small pool of water. "There's a leak."

"Is it serious?" Gary asked.

"There's no danger of a meltdown," Trent assured him.

A groan seemed to vibrate through the walls as if the place were haunted by a primitive spirit. Osato Goro was huddled in a corner. His eyes stared blankly at them, only the whites visible. Bald spots had already appeared on his skull and tufts of black hair littered his white smock. Bleeding gums dyed his teeth red, and his tongue curled back in his mouth like a shriveled serpent. A six-fingered hand was frozen into a claw that clutched his bullet-ravaged arm.

"Radiation poisoning," K.O. stated simply.

"What chance does he have?" Gary inquired.

"The exposure has been too great," Trent answered. "There's nothing anyone can do for him now. He'll die in agony within an hour."

"An appropriate end," K.O. remarked.

PHOENIX FORCE

AN EXECUTIONER SERIES

#5 The Fury Bombs

MORE GREAT ACTION COMING SOON!

The politics of terrorism had become too complicated for Seamus Dolan. He had a way to strike a blow at England that would be totally unexpected. And totally efficient.

Dolan was going to export his brand of terror to the United States and force a showdown with the British. Extortion and sabotage. Destruction and death. The scheme was daringly simple.

The White House and 10 Downing Street were soon united in the need for Mack Bolan's ultimate strength.

The Executioner's Phoenix Force deals in bullets, not blarney—they'll take a head shot before listening to any terrorist trash.

Move it, Phoenix, you're on your way!

Mack Bolan's

ABLE TEAM

AN EXECUTIONER SERIES

by Dick Stivers

In the fire-raking tradition of The Executioner, Able Team's Carl Lyons, Pol Blancanales and Gadgets Schwarz are the three hotshots who avenge terror with screaming silvered fury. They are the Death Squad reborn, and their long-awaited adventures are the best thing to happen since the Mack Bolan and the Phoenix Force series. Collect them all! They are classics of their kind! Do not miss these titles:

#1 Tower of Terror   **#3 Texas Showdown**
#2 The Hostaged Island   **#4 Amazon Slaughter**

WATCH FOR
Able Team #5: Cairo Countdown

Watch for new Able Team titles
wherever paperbacks are sold.

GOLD
EAGLE

MACK BOLAN

THE EXECUTIONER SERIES

Mack Bolan is the man who commands himself. He is the sniper-ideal: the executioner who knows the difference between duty and murder and can, when necessary, put to death methodically, unemotionally, and yet *personally*. Mack Bolan is the free world's leading force in the new Terrorist Wars, defying all terrorists and destroying them piece by piece, using his Vietnam-trained tactics and knowledge of jungle warfare. Bolan's new war is the most exciting series ever to explode into print. You won't want to miss a single word. Start your collection now!

"Highly successful" —*The New York Times*

#39 The New War
#40 Double Crossfire
#41 The Violent Streets
#42 The Iranian Hit
#43 Return to Vietnam
#44 Terrorist Summit
#45 Paramilitary Plot

#46 Bloodsport
#47 Renegade Agent
#48 The Libya Connection
#49 Doomsday Disciples
#50 Brothers in Blood
#51 Vulture's Vengeance

GOLD EAGLE

Available wherever paperbacks are sold.